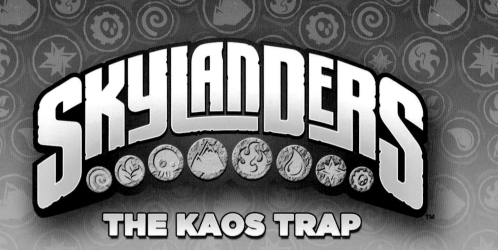

SKYLANDERS

THE KAOS TRAP

THE TRAP MASTERS

Story by:
DAVID A. RODRIGUEZ, ALEX NESS and **MICHAEL GRAHAM**
Written by:
DAVID A. RODRIGUEZ
Art by:
MIKE BOWDEN
Colors by:
DAVID GARCIA CRUZ
Letters by:
DERON BENNETT & TOM B. LONG
Edited by:
DAVID HEDGECOCK

 Spotlight

ABDOPUBLISHING.COM

Reinforced library bound edition published in 2016 by Spotlight,
a division of ABDO, PO Box 398166, Minneapolis, Minnesota 55439.
Spotlight produces high-quality reinforced library bound editions for
schools and libraries. Published by agreement with IDW.

Printed in the United States of America, North Mankato, Minnesota.
042015
092015

THIS BOOK CONTAINS
RECYCLED MATERIALS

SKYLANDERS: THE KAOS TRAP. OCTOBER 2014. FIRST PRINTING.
© 2015 Activision Publishing, Inc. SKYLANDERS and ACTIVISION are
registered trademarks of Activision Publishing, Inc. The IDW logo is registered
in the U.S. Patent and Trademark Office. IDW Publishing, a division of Idea and
Design Works, LLC. Editorial offices: 5080 Santa Fe Street, San Diego CA 92109. Any
similarities to persons living or dead are purely coincidental. With the exception of
artwork used for review purposes, none of the contents of this publication may be
reprinted without the permission of Idea and Design Works, LLC.

LIBRARY OF CONGRESS CATALOGING-IN-PUBLICATION DATA

Rodriguez, David A., author.
 The trap masters / writer: David A. Rodriguez, Alex Ness, and Michael Graham ;
artist: Mike Bowden ; colors: David Garcia Cruz.
    pages cm. -- (Skylanders: the kaos trap)
 Summary: "When Kaos commands his trolls and a doom raider to attack the Radiant
Isle, the Trap Team is called in for assistance. But is attacking the Radiant Isle really his
master plan?"-- Provided by publisher.
 ISBN 978-1-61479-387-8
1. Graphic novels. I. Bowden, Mike, illustrator. II. Skylanders (Game) III. Title.
PZ7.7.R6378Tr 2016
741.5'973--dc23
                              2015001613

Spotlight
A Division of ABDO
abdopublishing.com

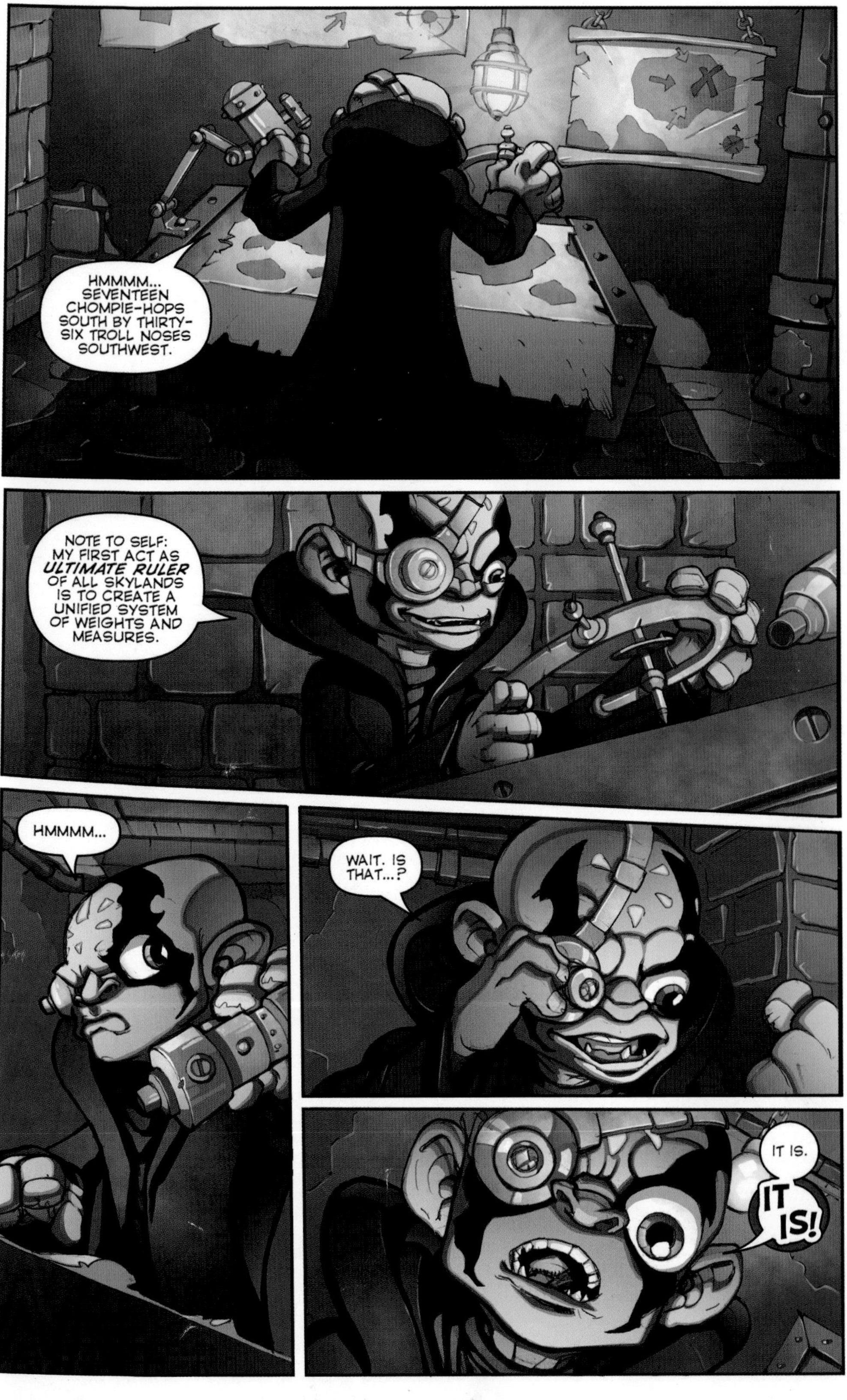
HMMMM... SEVENTEEN CHOMPIE-HOPS SOUTH BY THIRTY-SIX TROLL NOSES SOUTHWEST.
NOTE TO SELF: MY FIRST ACT AS *ULTIMATE RULER* OF ALL SKYLANDS IS TO CREATE A UNIFIED SYSTEM OF WEIGHTS AND MEASURES.
HMMMM...
WAIT. IS THAT...?
IT IS.
IT IS!

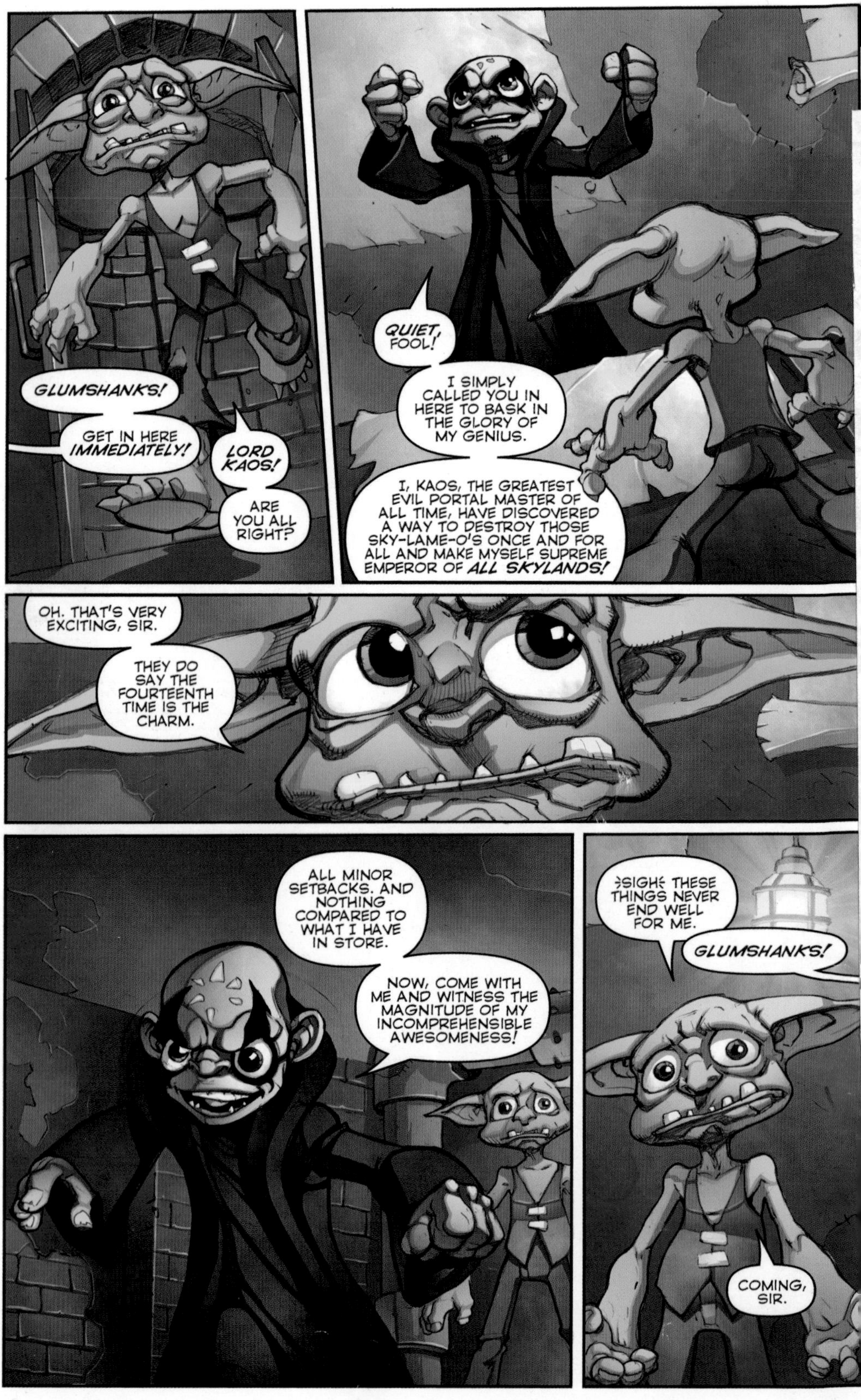
GLUMSHANKS!
GET IN HERE IMMEDIATELY!
LORD KAOS!
ARE YOU ALL RIGHT?
QUIET, FOOL!
I SIMPLY CALLED YOU IN HERE TO BASK IN THE GLORY OF MY GENIUS.
I, KAOS, THE GREATEST EVIL PORTAL MASTER OF ALL TIME, HAVE DISCOVERED A WAY TO DESTROY THOSE SKY-LAME-O'S ONCE AND FOR ALL AND MAKE MYSELF SUPREME EMPEROR OF ALL SKYLANDS!
OH. THAT'S VERY EXCITING, SIR.
THEY DO SAY THE FOURTEENTH TIME IS THE CHARM.
ALL MINOR SETBACKS. AND NOTHING COMPARED TO WHAT I HAVE IN STORE.
NOW, COME WITH ME AND WITNESS THE MAGNITUDE OF MY INCOMPREHENSIBLE AWESOMENESS!
SIGH THESE THINGS NEVER END WELL FOR ME.
GLUMSHANKS!
COMING, SIR.

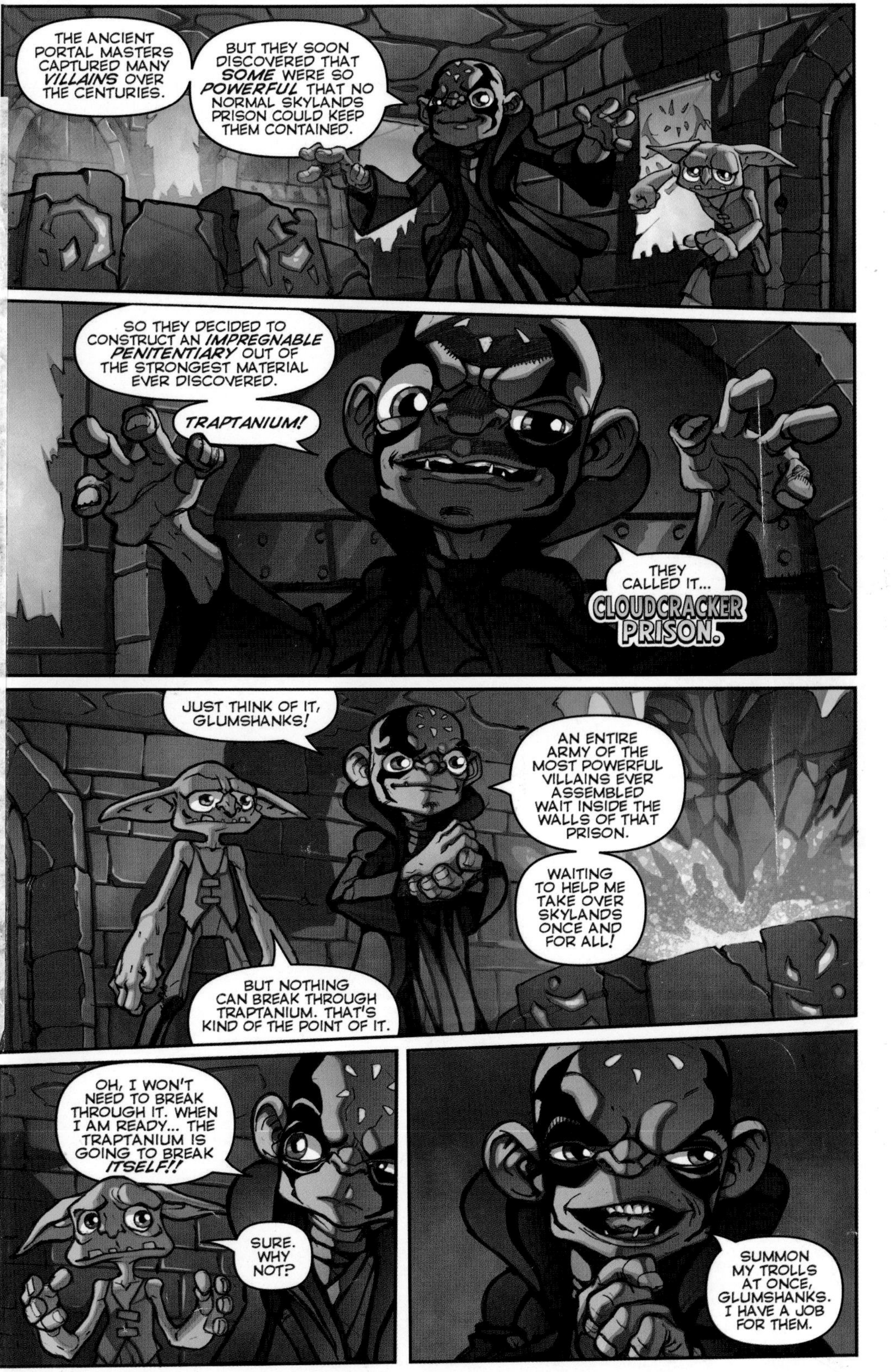
THE ANCIENT PORTAL MASTERS CAPTURED MANY VILLAINS OVER THE CENTURIES.
BUT THEY SOON DISCOVERED THAT SOME WERE SO POWERFUL THAT NO NORMAL SKYLANDS PRISON COULD KEEP THEM CONTAINED.
SO THEY DECIDED TO CONSTRUCT AN IMPREGNABLE PENITENTIARY OUT OF THE STRONGEST MATERIAL EVER DISCOVERED.
TRAPTANIUM!
THEY CALLED IT...
CLOUDCRACKER PRISON.
JUST THINK OF IT, GLUMSHANKS!
AN ENTIRE ARMY OF THE MOST POWERFUL VILLAINS EVER ASSEMBLED WAIT INSIDE THE WALLS OF THAT PRISON.
WAITING TO HELP ME TAKE OVER SKYLANDS ONCE AND FOR ALL!
BUT NOTHING CAN BREAK THROUGH TRAPTANIUM. THAT'S KIND OF THE POINT OF IT.
OH, I WON'T NEED TO BREAK THROUGH IT. WHEN I AM READY... THE TRAPTANIUM IS GOING TO BREAK ITSELF!!
SURE. WHY NOT?
SUMMON MY TROLLS AT ONCE, GLUMSHANKS. I HAVE A JOB FOR THEM.

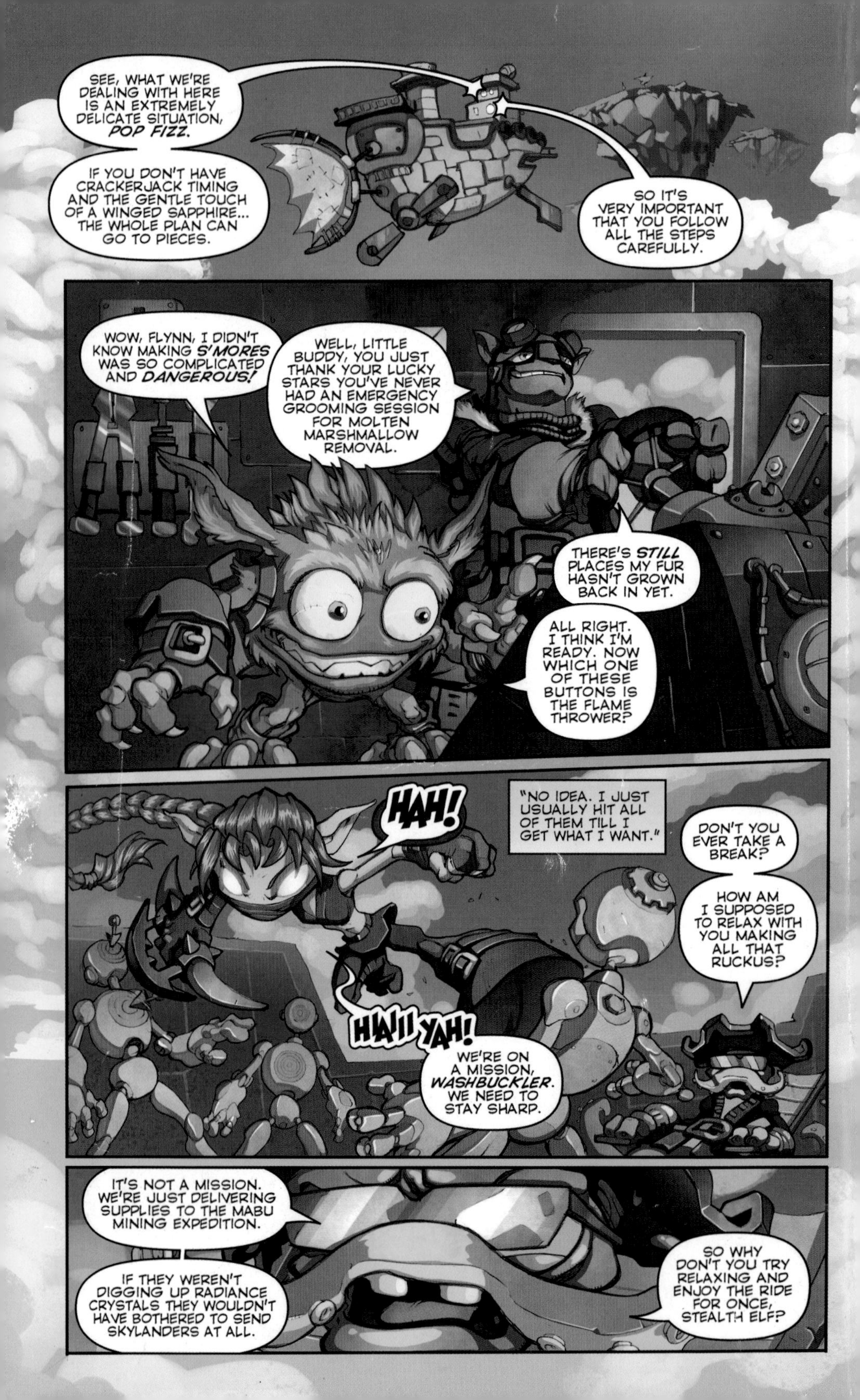
SEE, WHAT WE'RE DEALING WITH HERE IS AN EXTREMELY DELICATE SITUATION, POP FIZZ.
IF YOU DON'T HAVE CRACKERJACK TIMING AND THE GENTLE TOUCH OF A WINGED SAPPHIRE... THE WHOLE PLAN CAN GO TO PIECES.
SO IT'S VERY IMPORTANT THAT YOU FOLLOW ALL THE STEPS CAREFULLY.
WOW, FLYNN, I DIDN'T KNOW MAKING S'MORES WAS SO COMPLICATED AND DANGEROUS!
WELL, LITTLE BUDDY, YOU JUST THANK YOUR LUCKY STARS YOU'VE NEVER HAD AN EMERGENCY GROOMING SESSION FOR MOLTEN MARSHMALLOW REMOVAL.
THERE'S STILL PLACES MY FUR HASN'T GROWN BACK IN YET.
ALL RIGHT. I THINK I'M READY. NOW WHICH ONE OF THESE BUTTONS IS THE FLAME THROWER?
"NO IDEA. I JUST USUALLY HIT ALL OF THEM TILL I GET WHAT I WANT."
HAH!
DON'T YOU EVER TAKE A BREAK?
HOW AM I SUPPOSED TO RELAX WITH YOU MAKING ALL THAT RUCKUS?
HAJIII YAH!
WE'RE ON A MISSION, WASHBUCKLER. WE NEED TO STAY SHARP.
IT'S NOT A MISSION. WE'RE JUST DELIVERING SUPPLIES TO THE MABU MINING EXPEDITION.
IF THEY WEREN'T DIGGING UP RADIANCE CRYSTALS THEY WOULDN'T HAVE BOTHERED TO SEND SKYLANDERS AT ALL.
SO WHY DON'T YOU TRY RELAXING AND ENJOY THE RIDE FOR ONCE, STEALTH ELF?

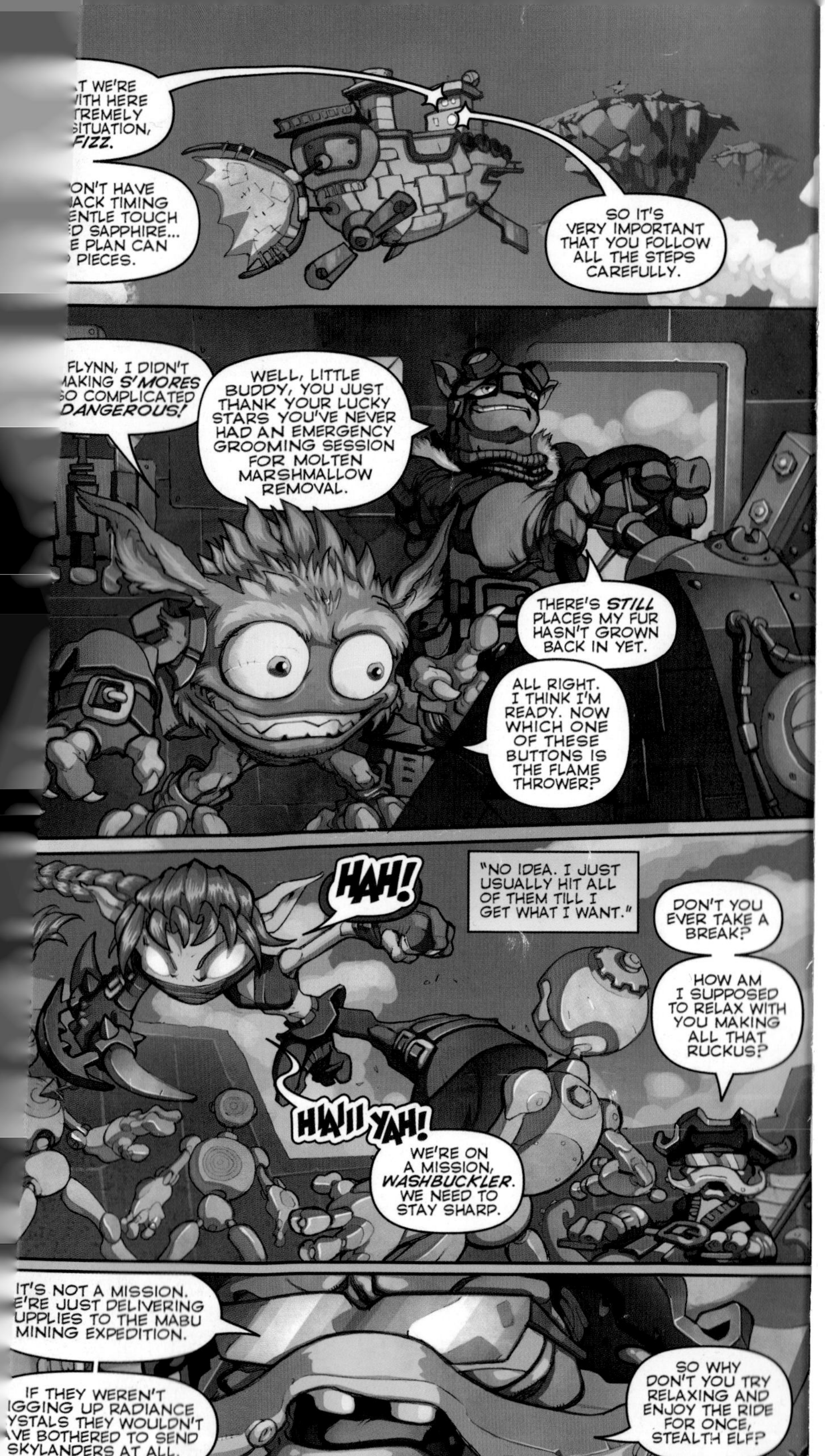

AT WE'RE WITH HERE TREMELY SITUATION, FIZZ.
ON'T HAVE ACK TIMING ENTLE TOUCH ED SAPPHIRE... E PLAN CAN PIECES.
SO IT'S VERY IMPORTANT THAT YOU FOLLOW ALL THE STEPS CAREFULLY.
FLYNN, I DIDN'T MAKING S'MORES SO COMPLICATED DANGEROUS!
WELL, LITTLE BUDDY, YOU JUST THANK YOUR LUCKY STARS YOU'VE NEVER HAD AN EMERGENCY GROOMING SESSION FOR MOLTEN MARSHMALLOW REMOVAL.
THERE'S STILL PLACES MY FUR HASN'T GROWN BACK IN YET.
ALL RIGHT. I THINK I'M READY. NOW WHICH ONE OF THESE BUTTONS IS THE FLAME THROWER?
HAH!
"NO IDEA. I JUST USUALLY HIT ALL OF THEM TILL I GET WHAT I WANT."
DON'T YOU EVER TAKE A BREAK?
HOW AM I SUPPOSED TO RELAX WITH YOU MAKING ALL THAT RUCKUS?
HIAII YAH!
WE'RE ON A MISSION, WASHBUCKLER. WE NEED TO STAY SHARP.
IT'S NOT A MISSION. E'RE JUST DELIVERING UPPLIES TO THE MABU MINING EXPEDITION.
IF THEY WEREN'T IGGING UP RADIANCE YSTALS THEY WOULDN'T AVE BOTHERED TO SEND SKYLANDERS AT ALL.
SO WHY DON'T YOU TRY RELAXING AND ENJOY THE RIDE FOR ONCE, STEALTH ELF?

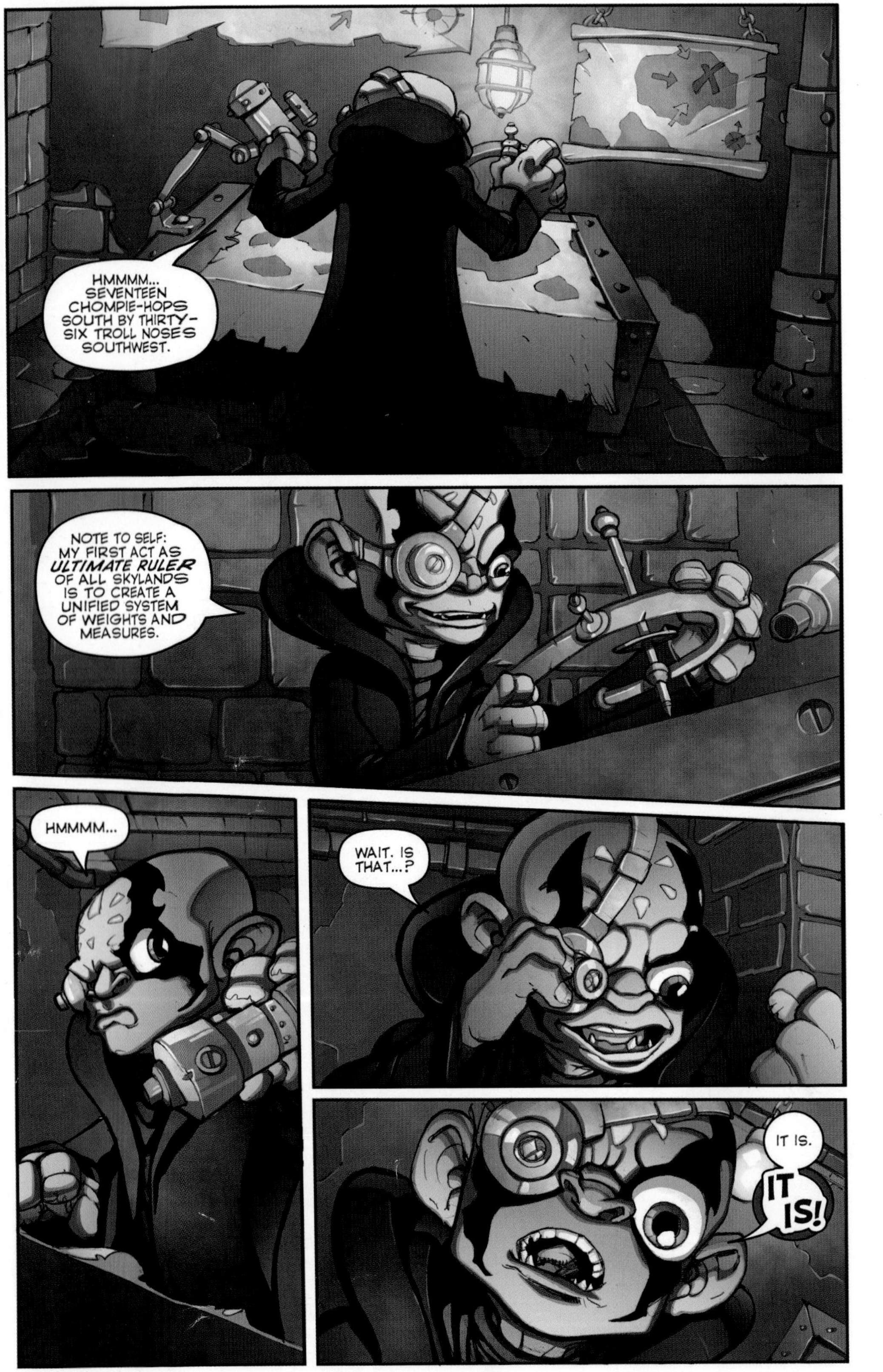

HMMMM... SEVENTEEN CHOMPIE-HOPS SOUTH BY THIRTY-SIX TROLL NOSES SOUTHWEST.
NOTE TO SELF: MY FIRST ACT AS ULTIMATE RULER OF ALL SKYLANDS IS TO CREATE A UNIFIED SYSTEM OF WEIGHTS AND MEASURES.
HMMMM...
WAIT. IS THAT...?
IT IS.
IT IS!

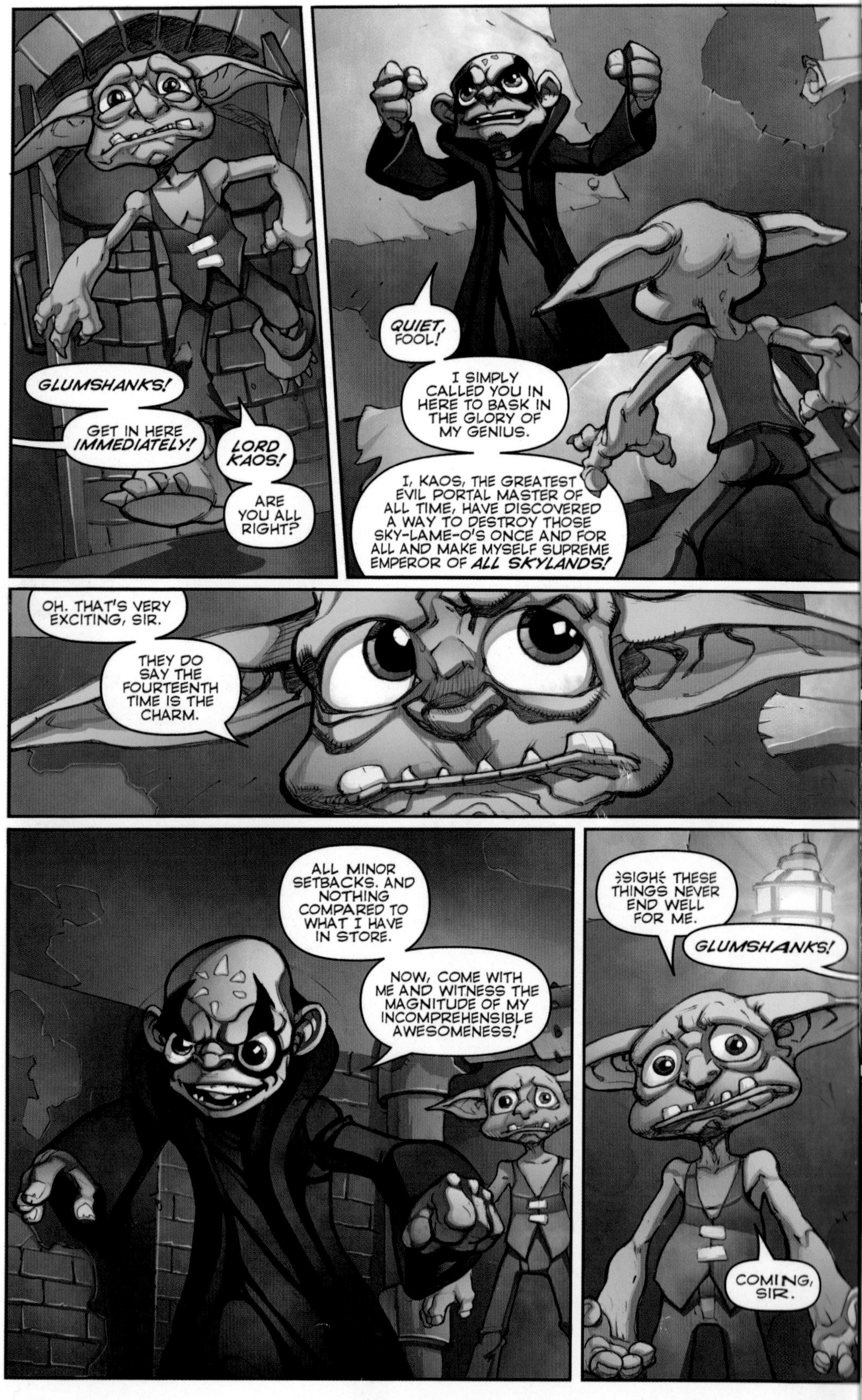
GLUMSHANKS!
GET IN HERE IMMEDIATELY!
LORD KAOS!
ARE YOU ALL RIGHT?
QUIET, FOOL!
I SIMPLY CALLED YOU IN HERE TO BASK IN THE GLORY OF MY GENIUS.
I, KAOS, THE GREATEST EVIL PORTAL MASTER OF ALL TIME, HAVE DISCOVERED A WAY TO DESTROY THOSE SKY-LAME-O'S ONCE AND FOR ALL AND MAKE MYSELF SUPREME EMPEROR OF ALL SKYLANDS!
OH. THAT'S VERY EXCITING, SIR.
THEY DO SAY THE FOURTEENTH TIME IS THE CHARM.
ALL MINOR SETBACKS. AND NOTHING COMPARED TO WHAT I HAVE IN STORE.
NOW, COME WITH ME AND WITNESS THE MAGNITUDE OF MY INCOMPREHENSIBLE AWESOMENESS!
SIGH THESE THINGS NEVER END WELL FOR ME.
GLUMSHANKS!
COMING, SIR.
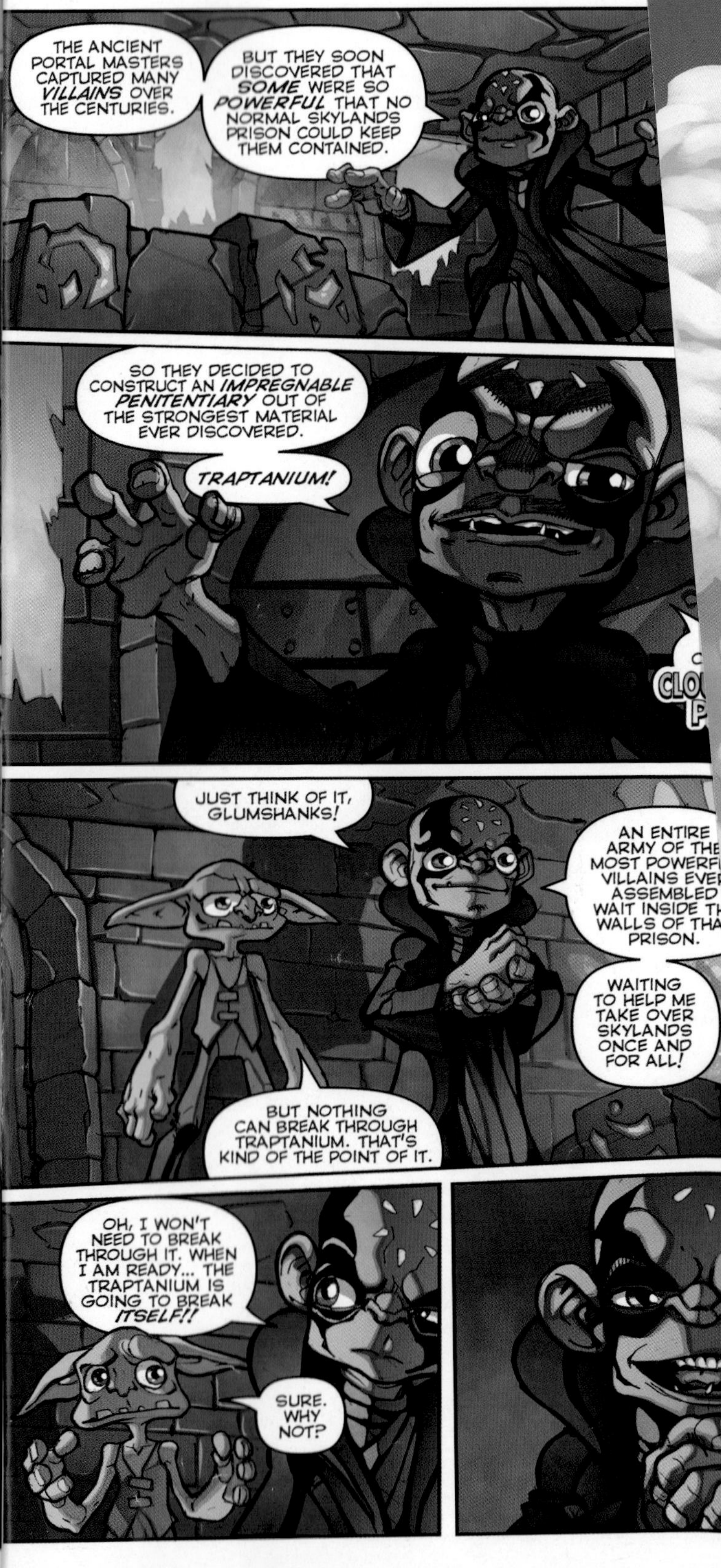
THE ANCIENT PORTAL MASTERS CAPTURED MANY VILLAINS OVER THE CENTURIES.
BUT THEY SOON DISCOVERED THAT SOME WERE SO POWERFUL THAT NO NORMAL SKYLANDS PRISON COULD KEEP THEM CONTAINED.
SO THEY DECIDED TO CONSTRUCT AN IMPREGNABLE PENITENTIARY OUT OF THE STRONGEST MATERIAL EVER DISCOVERED.
TRAPTANIUM!
JUST THINK OF IT, GLUMSHANKS!
WAITING TO HELP ME TAKE OVER SKYLANDS ONCE AND FOR ALL!
BUT NOTHING CAN BREAK THROUGH TRAPTANIUM. THAT'S KIND OF THE POINT OF IT.
OH, I WON'T NEED TO BREAK THROUGH IT. WHEN I AM READY... THE TRAPTANIUM IS GOING TO BREAK ITSELF!!
SURE. WHY NOT?

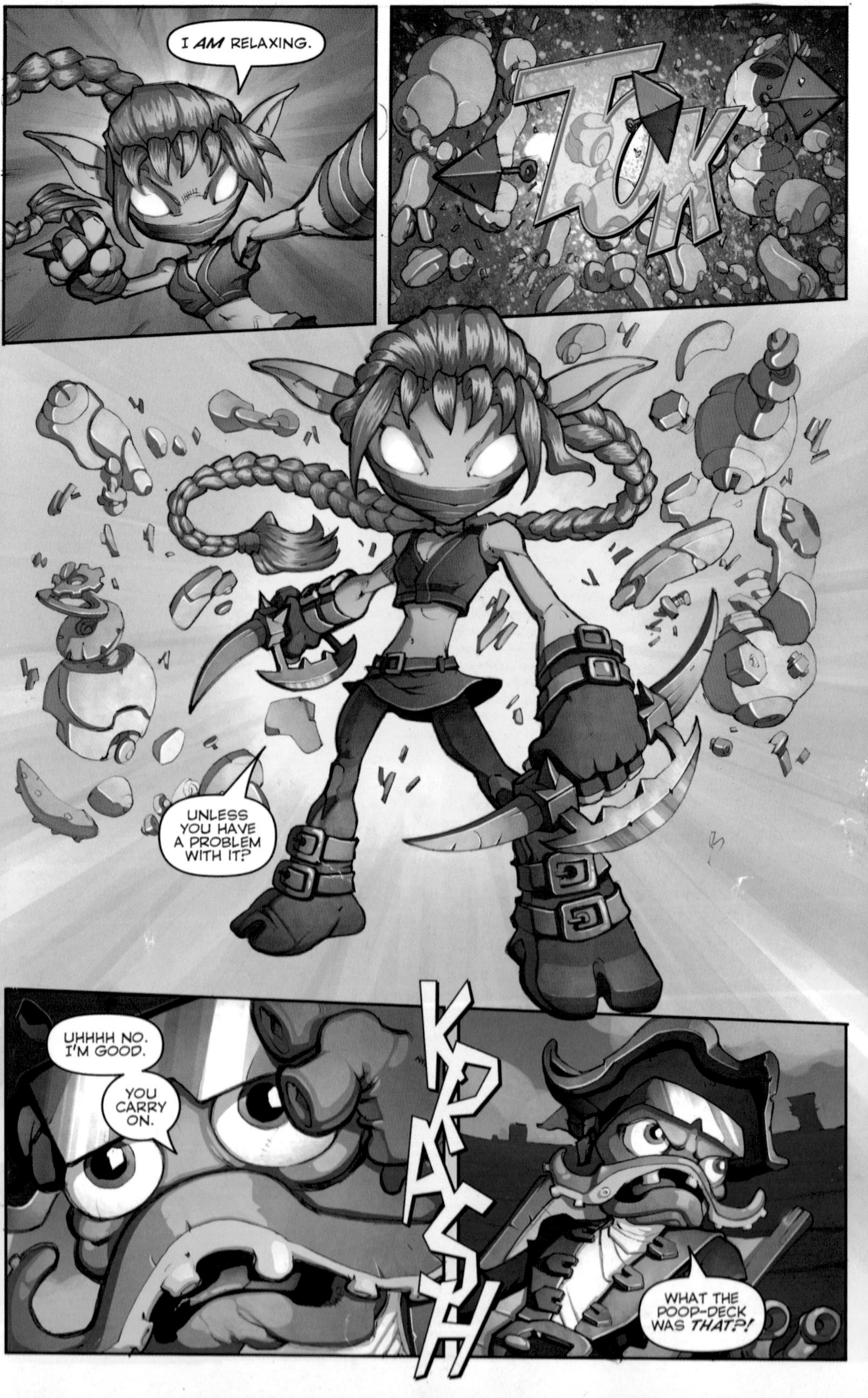
I AM RELAXING.
TUK
UNLESS YOU HAVE A PROBLEM WITH IT?
UHHHH NO. I'M GOOD.
YOU CARRY ON.
KRASH
WHAT THE POOP-DECK WAS THAT?!

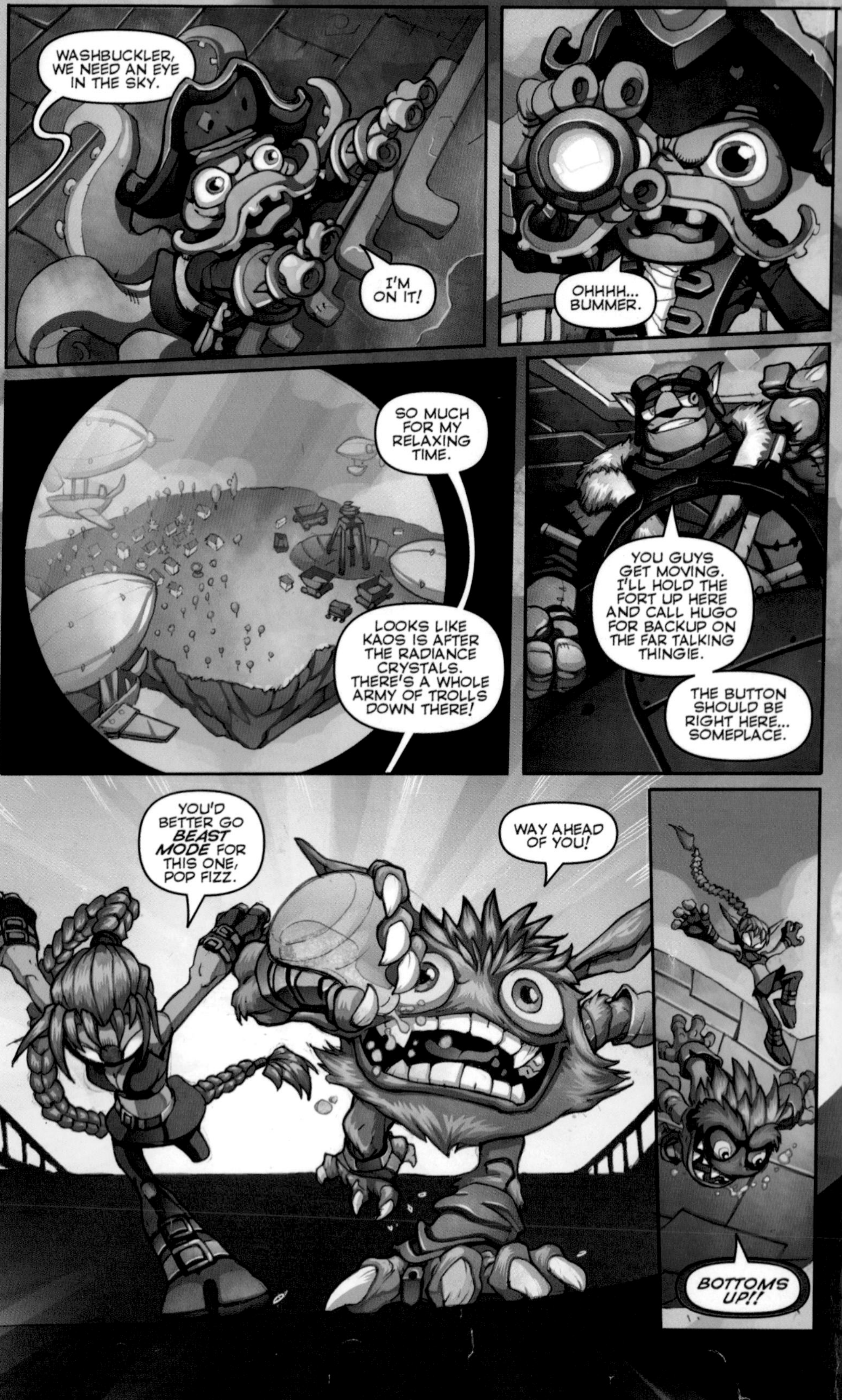
WASHBUCKLER, WE NEED AN EYE IN THE SKY.
I'M ON IT!
OHHHH... BUMMER.
SO MUCH FOR MY RELAXING TIME.
LOOKS LIKE KAOS IS AFTER THE RADIANCE CRYSTALS. THERE'S A WHOLE ARMY OF TROLLS DOWN THERE!
YOU GUYS GET MOVING. I'LL HOLD THE FORT UP HERE AND CALL HUGO FOR BACKUP ON THE FAR TALKING THINGIE.
THE BUTTON SHOULD BE RIGHT HERE... SOMEPLACE.
YOU'D BETTER GO *BEAST MODE* FOR THIS ONE, POP FIZZ.
WAY AHEAD OF YOU!
BOTTOMS UP!!

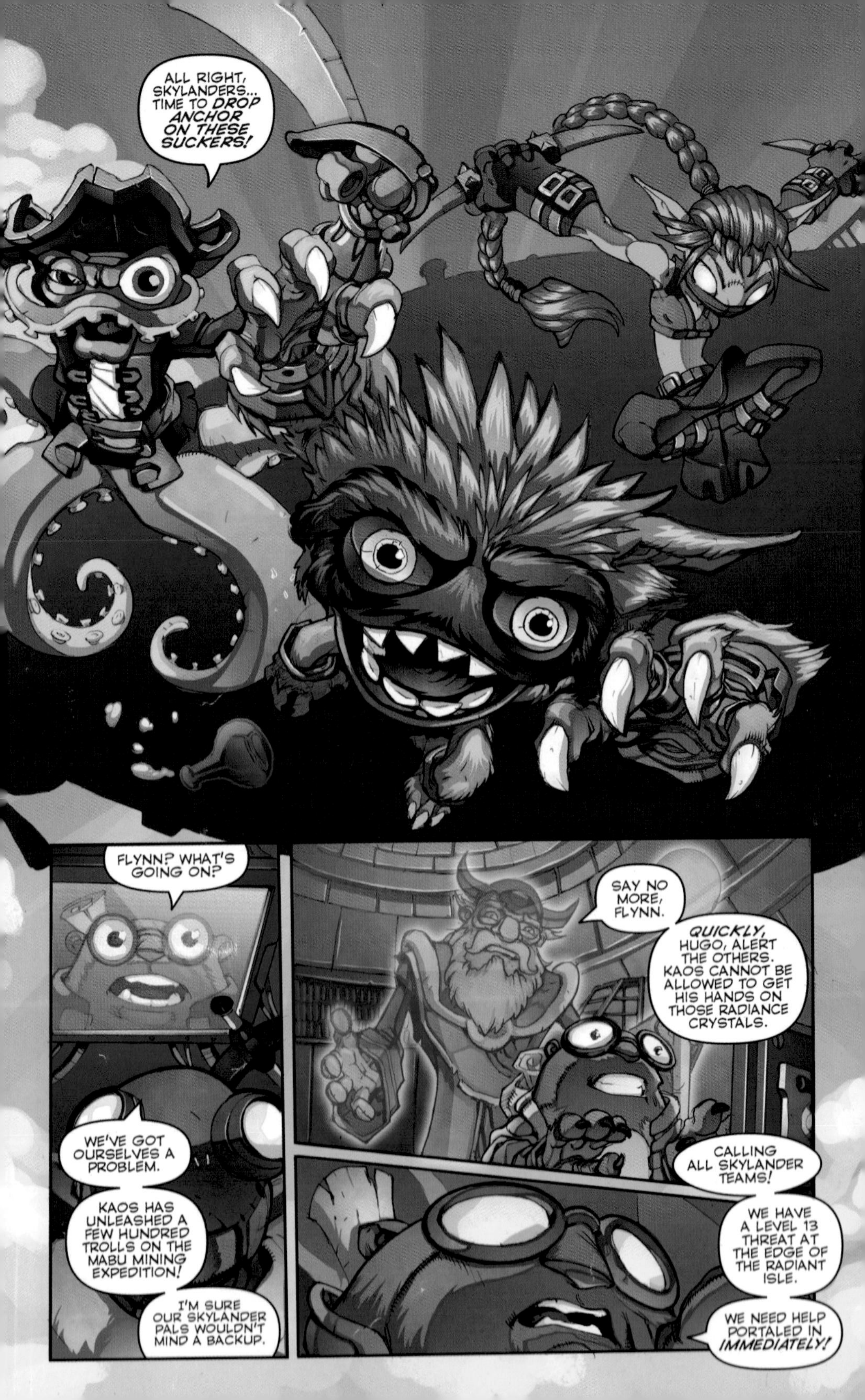

ALL RIGHT, SKYLANDERS... TIME TO *DROP ANCHOR ON THESE SUCKERS!*
FLYNN? WHAT'S GOING ON?
WE'VE GOT OURSELVES A PROBLEM.
KAOS HAS UNLEASHED A FEW HUNDRED TROLLS ON THE MABU MINING EXPEDITION!
I'M SURE OUR SKYLANDER PALS WOULDN'T MIND A BACKUP.
SAY NO MORE, FLYNN.
QUICKLY, HUGO, ALERT THE OTHERS. KAOS CANNOT BE ALLOWED TO GET HIS HANDS ON THOSE RADIANCE CRYSTALS.
CALLING ALL SKYLANDER TEAMS!
WE HAVE A LEVEL 13 THREAT AT THE EDGE OF THE RADIANT ISLE.
WE NEED HELP PORTALED IN *IMMEDIATELY!*

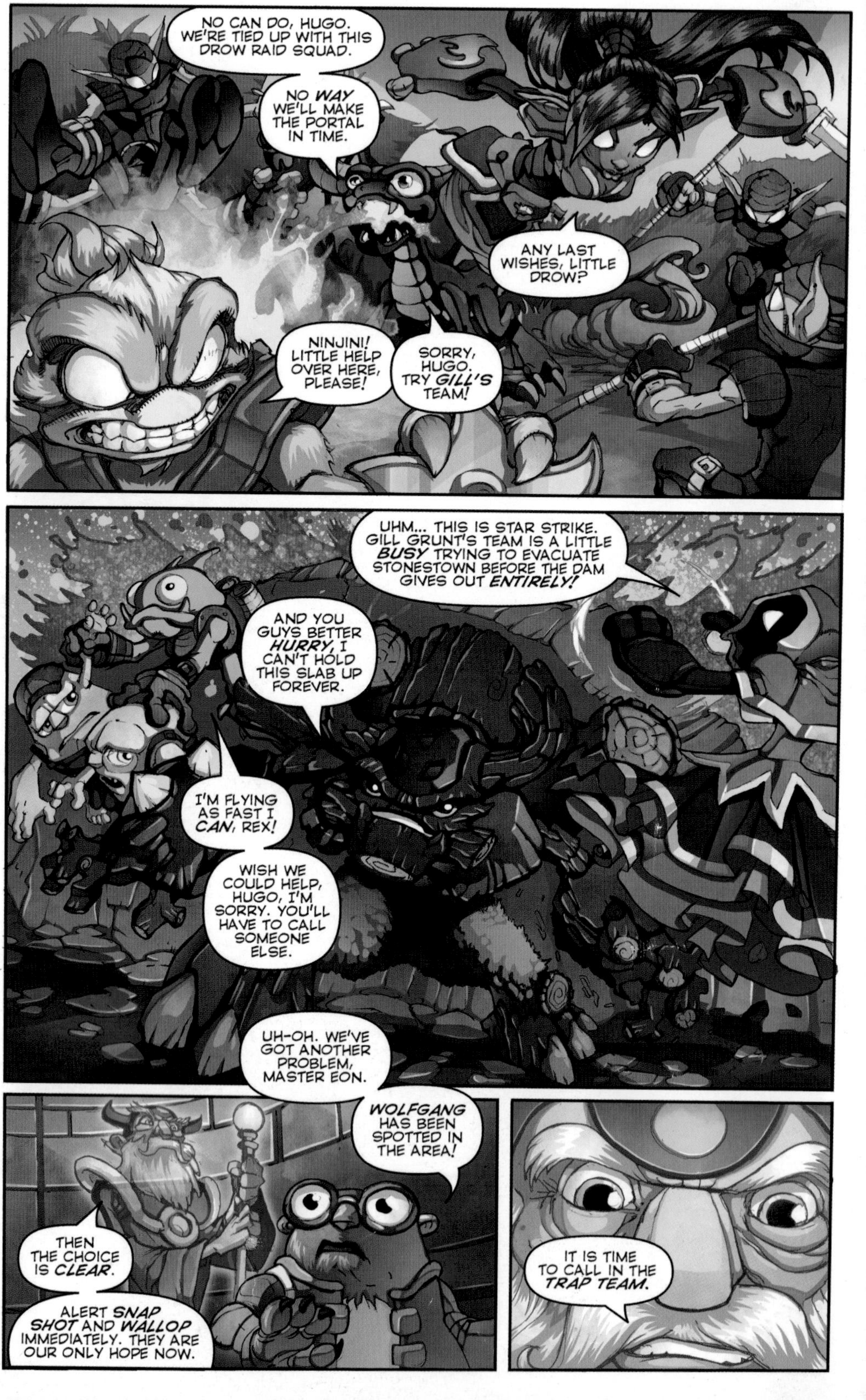
NO CAN DO, HUGO. WE'RE TIED UP WITH THIS DROW RAID SQUAD.
NO *WAY* WE'LL MAKE THE PORTAL IN TIME.
ANY LAST WISHES, LITTLE DROW?
NINJINI! LITTLE HELP OVER HERE, PLEASE!
SORRY, HUGO. TRY *GILL'S* TEAM!
UHM... THIS IS STAR STRIKE. GILL GRUNT'S TEAM IS A LITTLE *BUSY* TRYING TO EVACUATE STONESTOWN BEFORE THE DAM GIVES OUT *ENTIRELY!*
AND YOU GUYS BETTER *HURRY*, I CAN'T HOLD THIS SLAB UP FOREVER.
I'M FLYING AS FAST I *CAN*, REX!
WISH WE COULD HELP, HUGO, I'M SORRY. YOU'LL HAVE TO CALL SOMEONE ELSE.
UH-OH. WE'VE GOT ANOTHER PROBLEM, MASTER EON.
WOLFGANG HAS BEEN SPOTTED IN THE AREA!
THEN THE CHOICE IS *CLEAR*.
ALERT *SNAP SHOT* AND *WALLOP* IMMEDIATELY. THEY ARE OUR ONLY HOPE NOW.
IT IS TIME TO CALL IN THE *TRAP TEAM*.

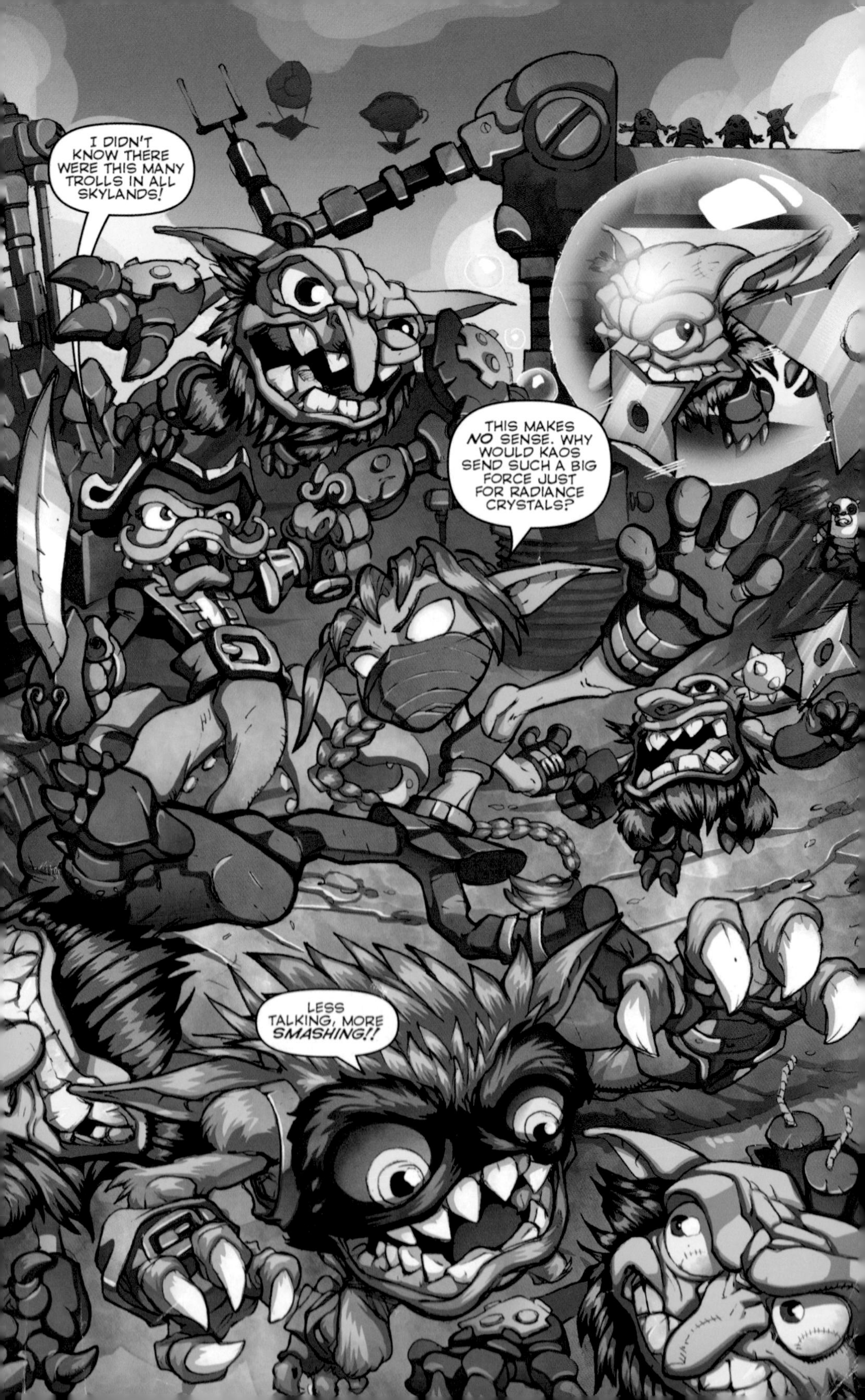
I DIDN'T KNOW THERE WERE THIS MANY TROLLS IN ALL SKYLANDS!
THIS MAKES *NO* SENSE. WHY WOULD KAOS SEND SUCH A BIG FORCE JUST FOR RADIANCE CRYSTALS?
LESS TALKING, MORE *SMASHING!!*

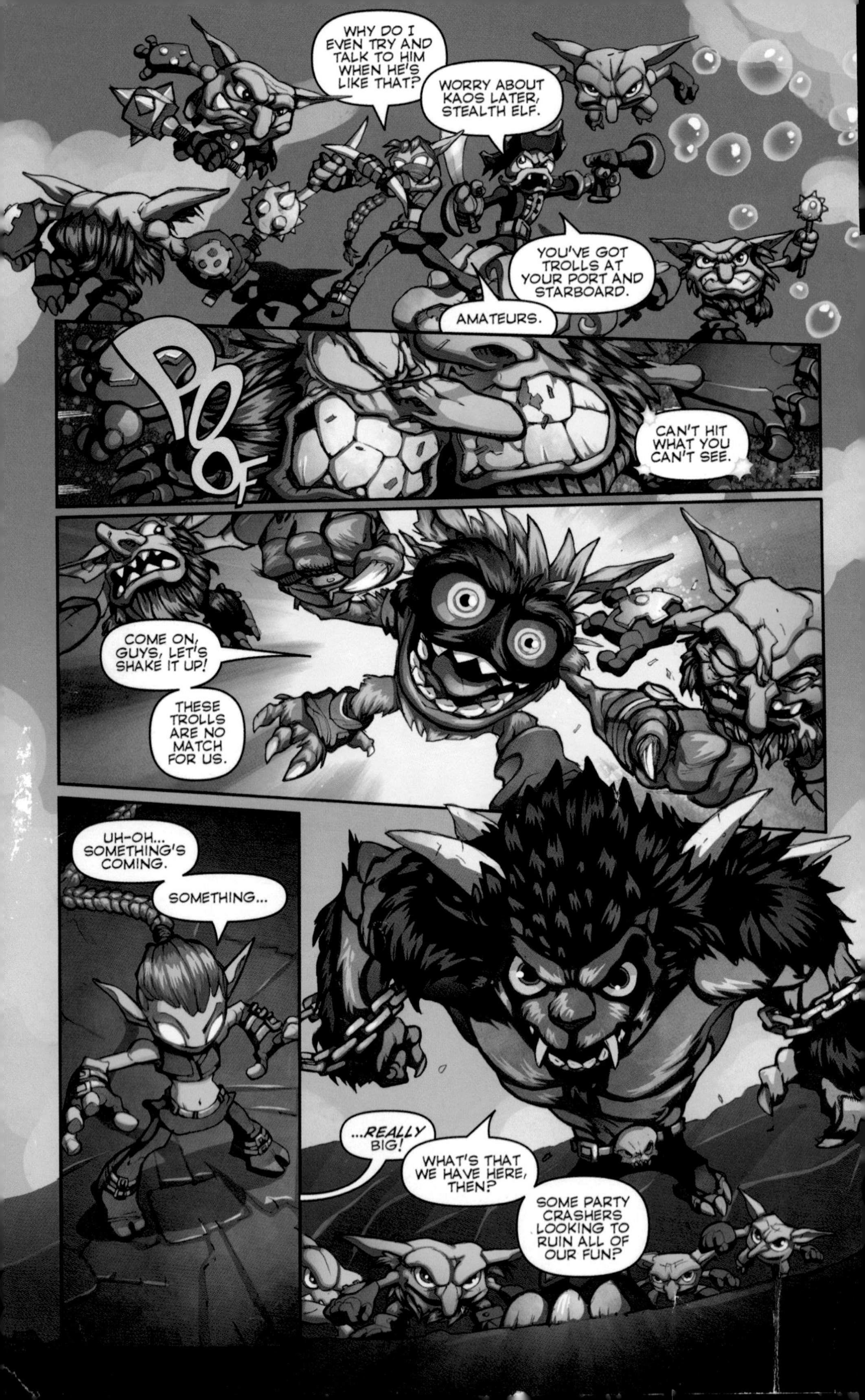
WHY DO I EVEN TRY AND TALK TO HIM WHEN HE'S LIKE THAT?
WORRY ABOUT KAOS LATER, STEALTH ELF.
YOU'VE GOT TROLLS AT YOUR PORT AND STARBOARD.
AMATEURS.
POOF
CAN'T HIT WHAT YOU CAN'T SEE.
COME ON, GUYS, LET'S SHAKE IT UP!
THESE TROLLS ARE NO MATCH FOR US.
UH-OH... SOMETHING'S COMING.
SOMETHING...
...*REALLY* BIG!
WHAT'S THAT WE HAVE HERE, THEN?
SOME PARTY CRASHERS LOOKING TO RUIN ALL OF OUR FUN?

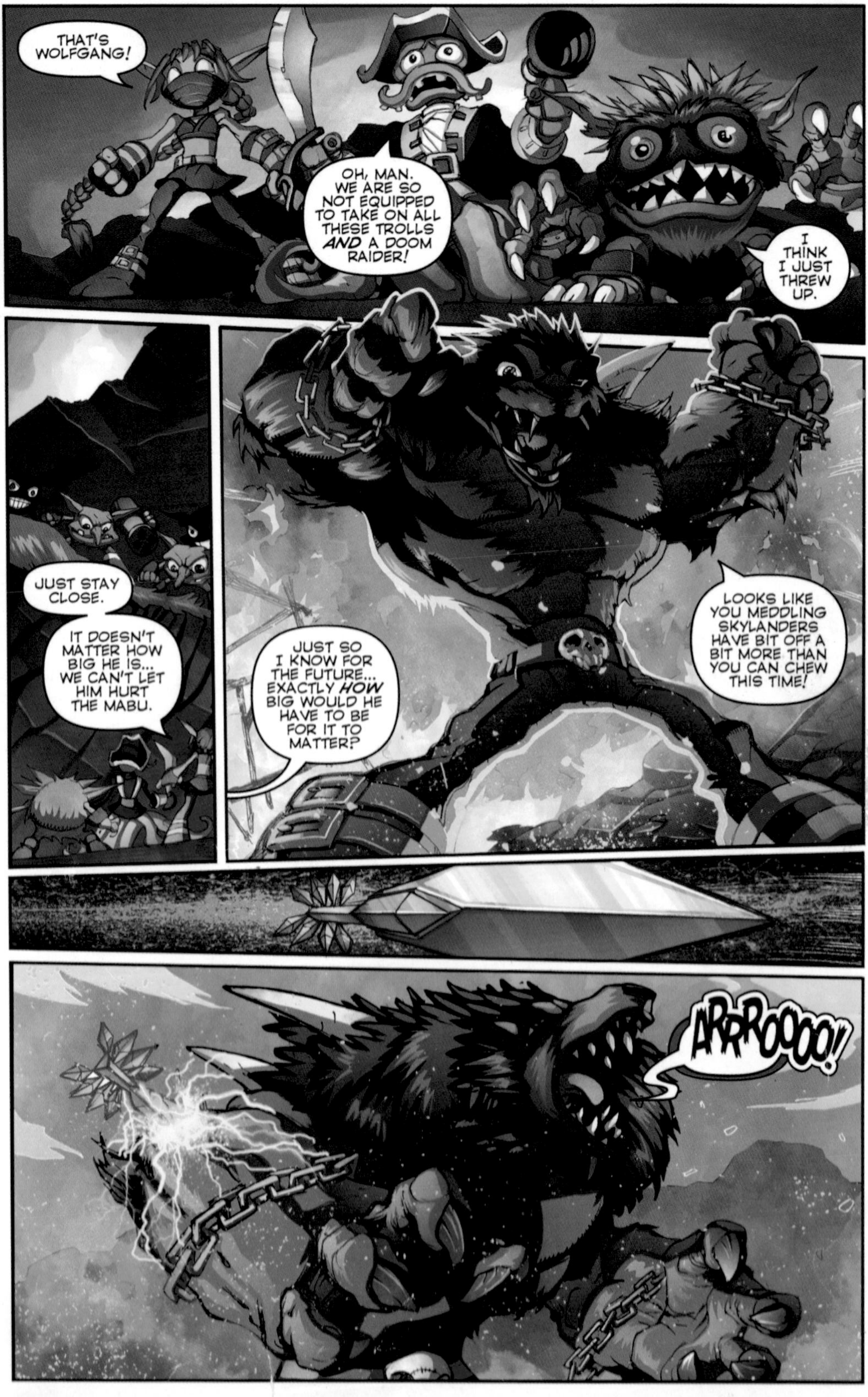
THAT'S WOLFGANG!
OH, MAN. WE ARE SO NOT EQUIPPED TO TAKE ON ALL THESE TROLLS AND A DOOM RAIDER!
I THINK I JUST THREW UP.
JUST STAY CLOSE.
IT DOESN'T MATTER HOW BIG HE IS... WE CAN'T LET HIM HURT THE MABU.
JUST SO I KNOW FOR THE FUTURE... EXACTLY HOW BIG WOULD HE HAVE TO BE FOR IT TO MATTER?
LOOKS LIKE YOU MEDDLING SKYLANDERS HAVE BIT OFF A BIT MORE THAN YOU CAN CHEW THIS TIME!
ARRROOOO!

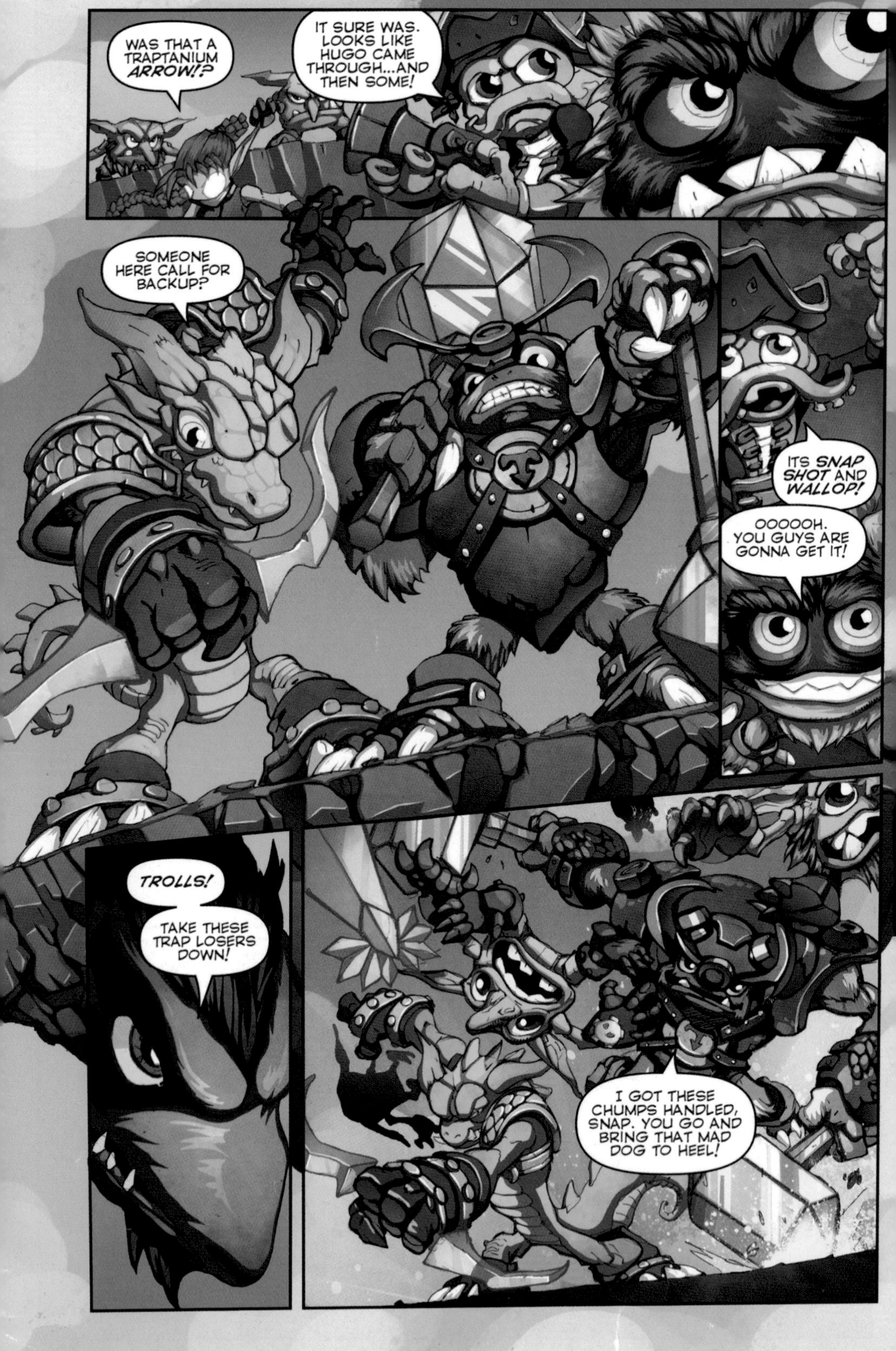

WAS THAT A TRAPTANIUM *ARROW!?*
IT SURE WAS. LOOKS LIKE HUGO CAME THROUGH...AND THEN SOME!
SOMEONE HERE CALL FOR BACKUP?
ITS *SNAP SHOT* AND *WALLOP!*
OOOOOH. YOU GUYS ARE GONNA GET IT!
TROLLS!
TAKE THESE TRAP LOSERS DOWN!
I GOT THESE CHUMPS HANDLED, SNAP. YOU GO AND BRING THAT MAD DOG TO HEEL!

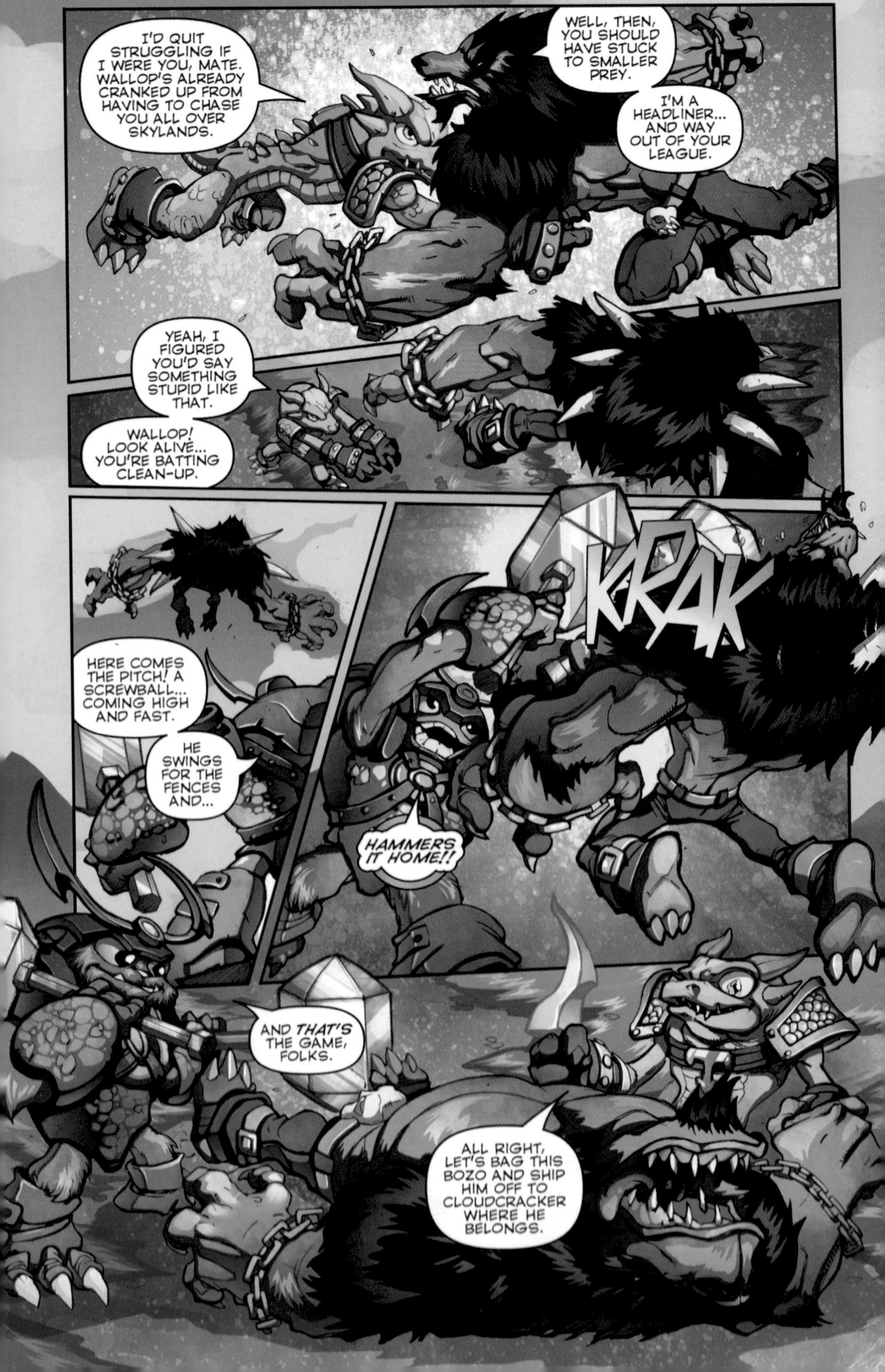
I'D QUIT STRUGGLING IF I WERE YOU, MATE. WALLOP'S ALREADY CRANKED UP FROM HAVING TO CHASE YOU ALL OVER SKYLANDS.
WELL, THEN, YOU SHOULD HAVE STUCK TO SMALLER PREY.
I'M A HEADLINER... AND WAY OUT OF YOUR LEAGUE.
YEAH, I FIGURED YOU'D SAY SOMETHING STUPID LIKE THAT.
WALLOP! LOOK ALIVE... YOU'RE BATTING CLEAN-UP.
HERE COMES THE PITCH! A SCREWBALL... COMING HIGH AND FAST.
HE SWINGS FOR THE FENCES AND...
KRAK
HAMMERS IT HOME!!
AND THAT'S THE GAME, FOLKS.
ALL RIGHT, LET'S BAG THIS BOZO AND SHIP HIM OFF TO CLOUDCRACKER WHERE HE BELONGS.

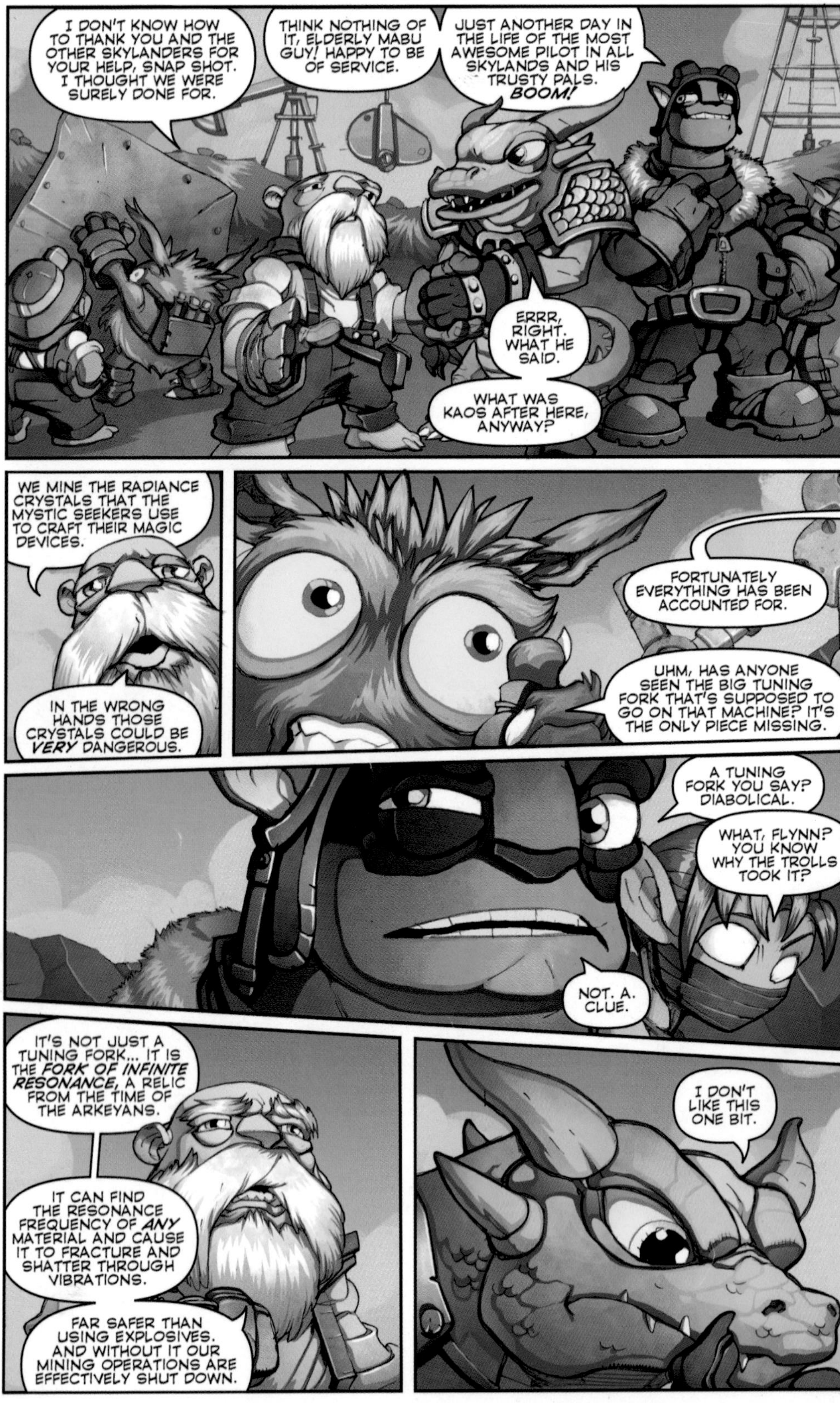

I DON'T KNOW HOW TO THANK YOU AND THE OTHER SKYLANDERS FOR YOUR HELP, SNAP SHOT. I THOUGHT WE WERE SURELY DONE FOR.
THINK NOTHING OF IT, ELDERLY MABU GUY! HAPPY TO BE OF SERVICE.
JUST ANOTHER DAY IN THE LIFE OF THE MOST AWESOME PILOT IN ALL SKYLANDS AND HIS TRUSTY PALS. *BOOM!*
ERRR, RIGHT. WHAT HE SAID.
WHAT WAS KAOS AFTER HERE, ANYWAY?
WE MINE THE RADIANCE CRYSTALS THAT THE MYSTIC SEEKERS USE TO CRAFT THEIR MAGIC DEVICES.
IN THE WRONG HANDS THOSE CRYSTALS COULD BE *VERY* DANGEROUS.
FORTUNATELY EVERYTHING HAS BEEN ACCOUNTED FOR.
UHM, HAS ANYONE SEEN THE BIG TUNING FORK THAT'S SUPPOSED TO GO ON THAT MACHINE? IT'S THE ONLY PIECE MISSING.
A TUNING FORK YOU SAY? DIABOLICAL.
WHAT, FLYNN? YOU KNOW WHY THE TROLLS TOOK IT?
NOT. A. CLUE.
IT'S NOT JUST A TUNING FORK... IT IS THE *FORK OF INFINITE RESONANCE*, A RELIC FROM THE TIME OF THE ARKEYANS.
IT CAN FIND THE RESONANCE FREQUENCY OF *ANY* MATERIAL AND CAUSE IT TO FRACTURE AND SHATTER THROUGH VIBRATIONS.
FAR SAFER THAN USING EXPLOSIVES. AND WITHOUT IT OUR MINING OPERATIONS ARE EFFECTIVELY SHUT DOWN.
I DON'T LIKE THIS ONE BIT.

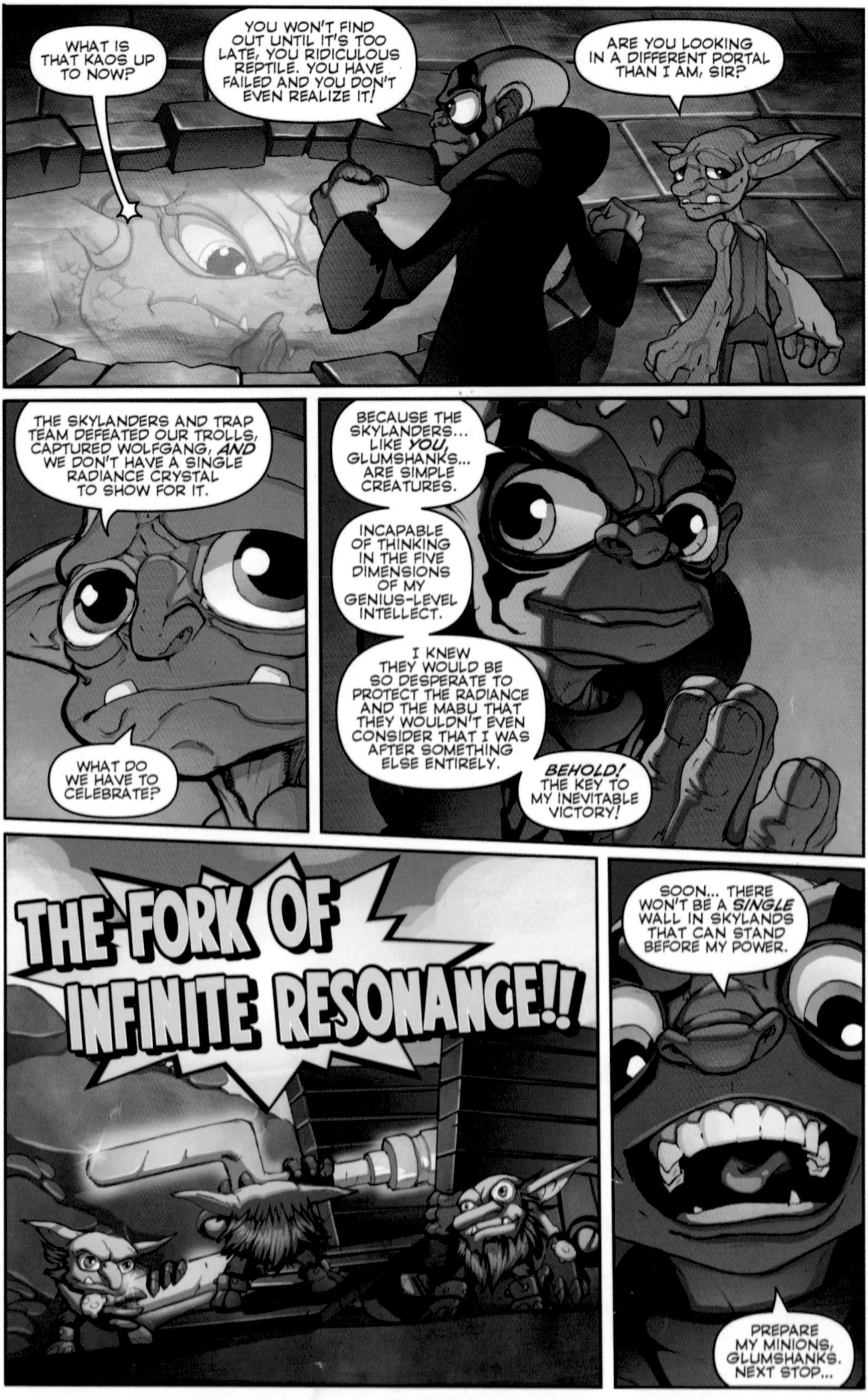

WHAT IS THAT KAOS UP TO NOW?
YOU WON'T FIND OUT UNTIL IT'S TOO LATE, YOU RIDICULOUS REPTILE. YOU HAVE FAILED AND YOU DON'T EVEN REALIZE IT!
ARE YOU LOOKING IN A DIFFERENT PORTAL THAN I AM, SIR?
THE SKYLANDERS AND TRAP TEAM DEFEATED OUR TROLLS, CAPTURED WOLFGANG, AND WE DON'T HAVE A SINGLE RADIANCE CRYSTAL TO SHOW FOR IT.
WHAT DO WE HAVE TO CELEBRATE?
BECAUSE THE SKYLANDERS... LIKE YOU, GLUMSHANKS... ARE SIMPLE CREATURES.
INCAPABLE OF THINKING IN THE FIVE DIMENSIONS OF MY GENIUS-LEVEL INTELLECT.
I KNEW THEY WOULD BE SO DESPERATE TO PROTECT THE RADIANCE AND THE MABU THAT THEY WOULDN'T EVEN CONSIDER THAT I WAS AFTER SOMETHING ELSE ENTIRELY.
BEHOLD! THE KEY TO MY INEVITABLE VICTORY!
THE FORK OF INFINITE RESONANCE!!
SOON... THERE WON'T BE A SINGLE WALL IN SKYLANDS THAT CAN STAND BEFORE MY POWER.
PREPARE MY MINIONS, GLUMSHANKS. NEXT STOP...

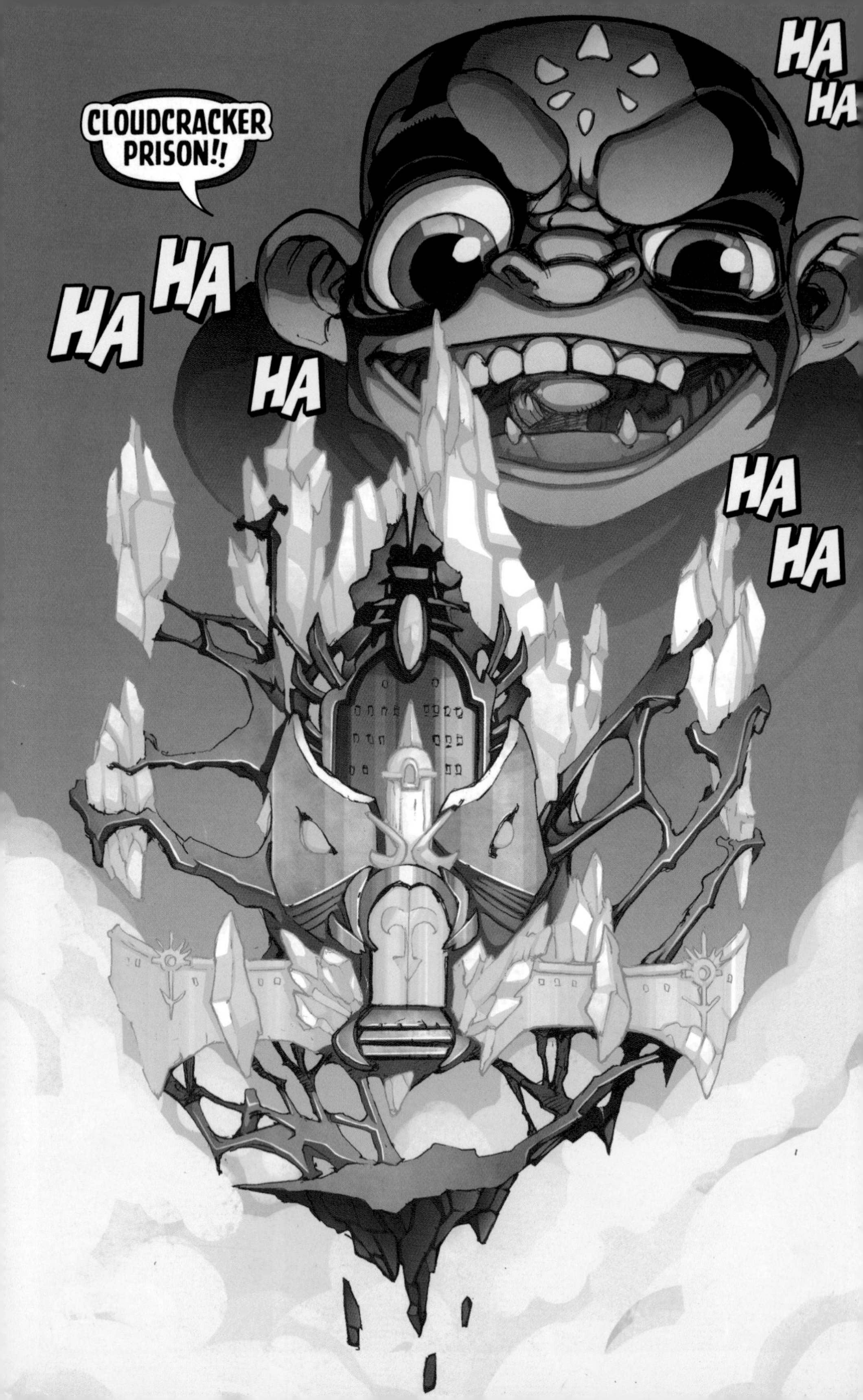
CLOUDCRACKER PRISON!!
HA HA
HA HA
HA
HA HA

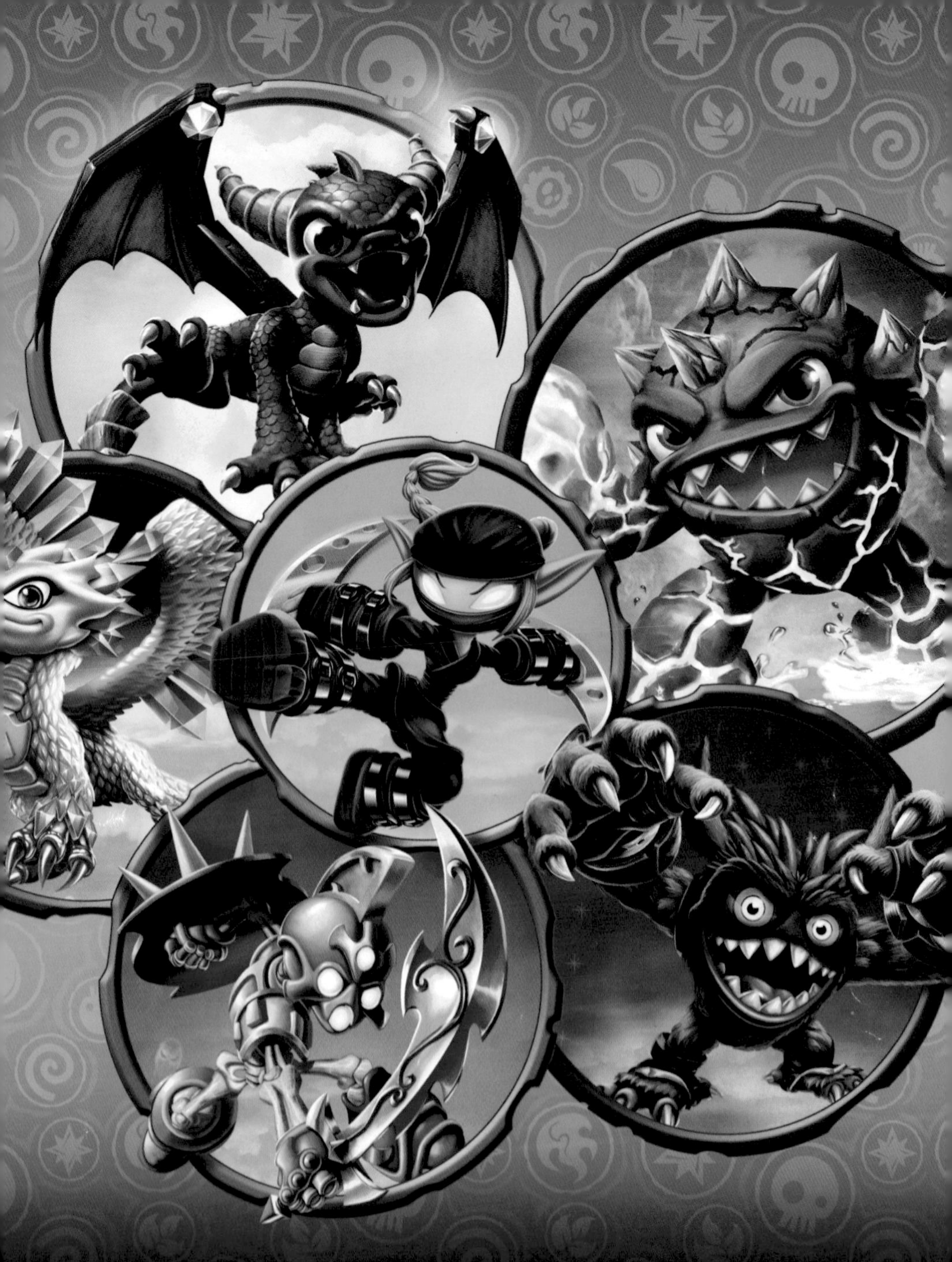

FOOD FIGHT

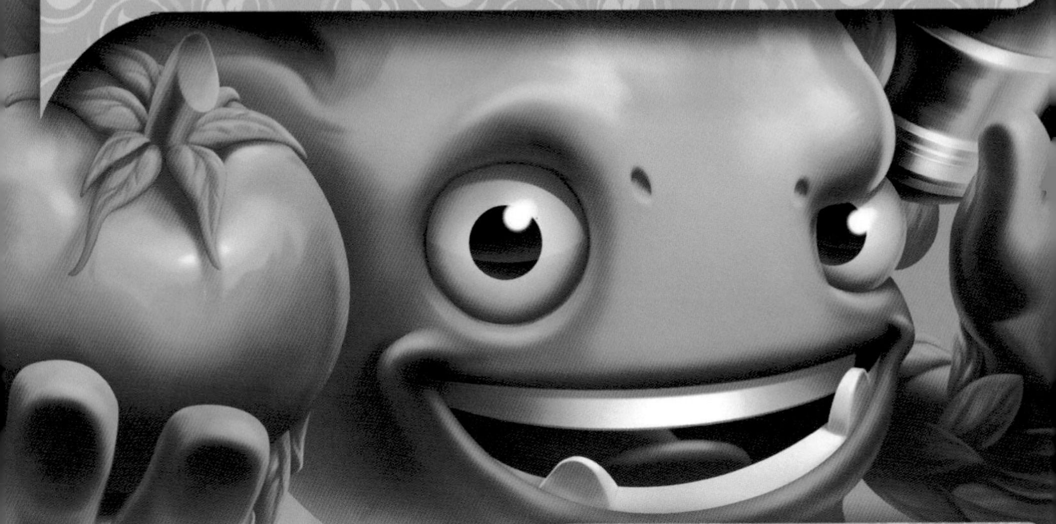

BIO

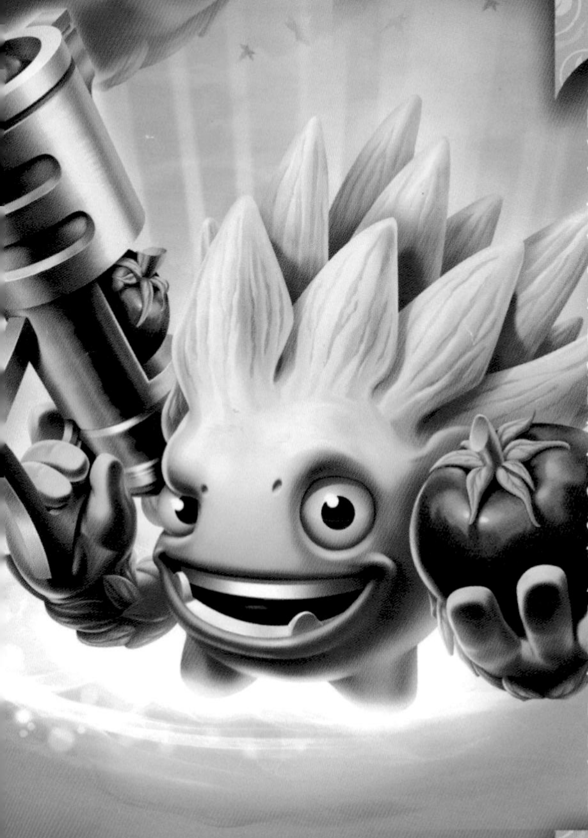

Food Fight does more than just play with his food, he battles with it! This tough little Veggie Warrior is the byproduct of a troll food experiment gone wrong. When the Troll Farmers Guild attempted to fertilize their soil with gunpowder, they got more than a super snack—they got an all-out Food Fight! Rising from the ground, he led the neighborhood Garden Patrol to victory. Later, he went on to defend his garden home against a rogue army of gnomes after they attempted to wrap the Asparagus people in bacon! His courage caught the eye of Master Eon, who decided that this was one veggie lover he needed on his side as a valued member of the Skylanders. When it comes to Food Fight, it's all you can eat for evil!

WILDFIRE

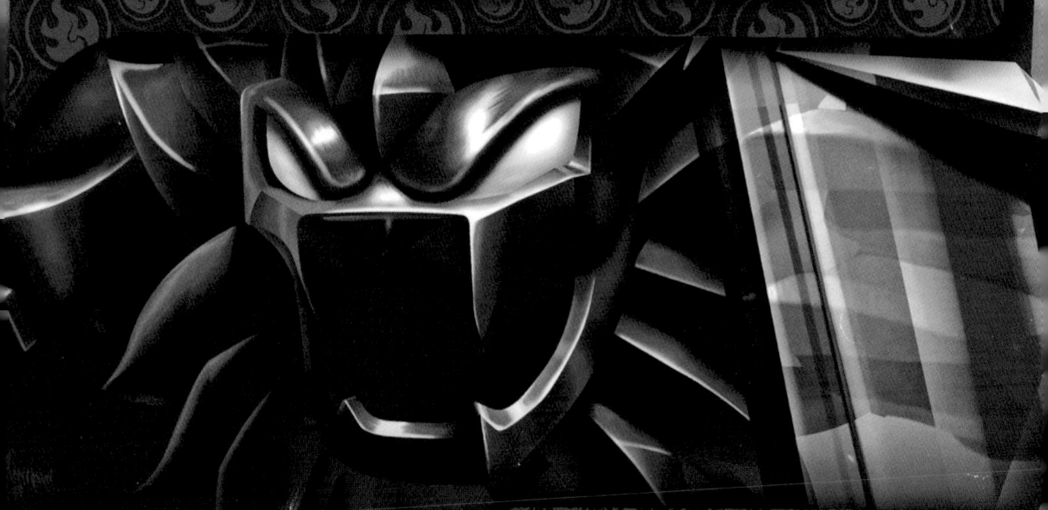

BIO

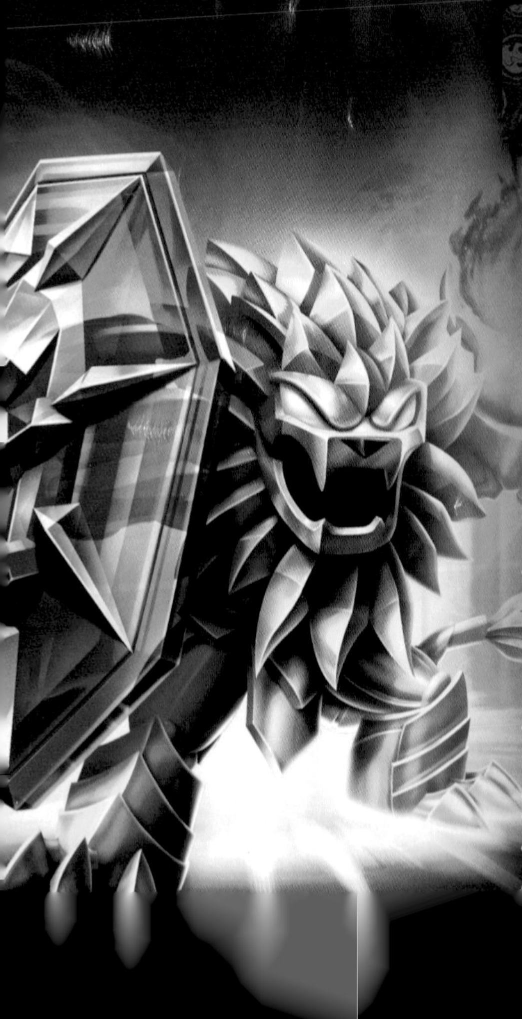

Wildfire was once a young lion of the Fire Claw Clan, about to enter into the Rite of Infernos—a test of survival in the treacherous fire plains. However, because he was made of gold, he was treated as an outcast and not allowed to participate. But this didn't stop him. That night, Wildfire secretly followed the path of the other lions, carrying only his father's enchanted shield. Soon he found them cornered by a giant flame scorpion. Using the shield, he protected the group from the beast's enormous stinging tail, giving them time to safely escape. And though Wildfire was injured in the fight, his father's shield magically changed him—magnifying the strength that was already in his heart—making him the mightiest of his clan. Now part of the Trap Team, Wildfire uses his enormous Traptanium-bonded shield to defend any and all who need it!

SNAP SHOT

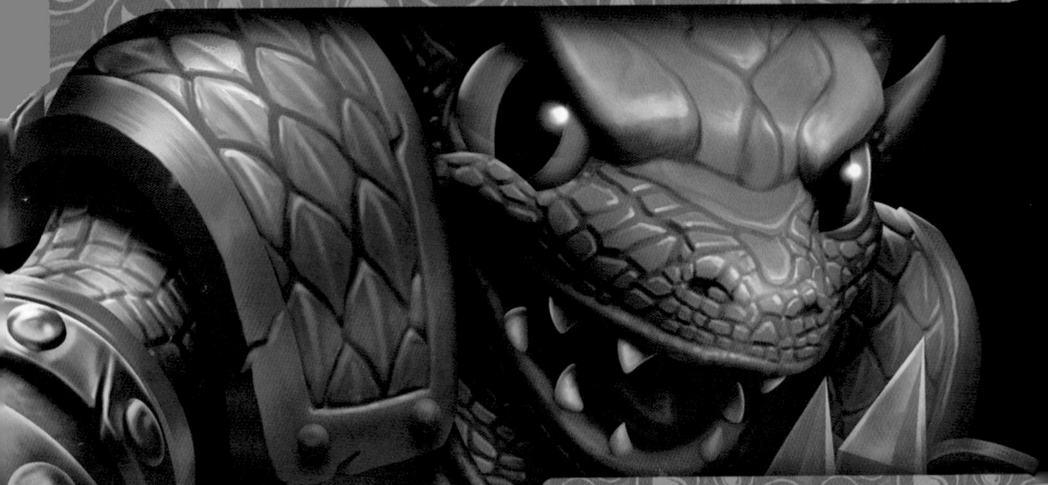

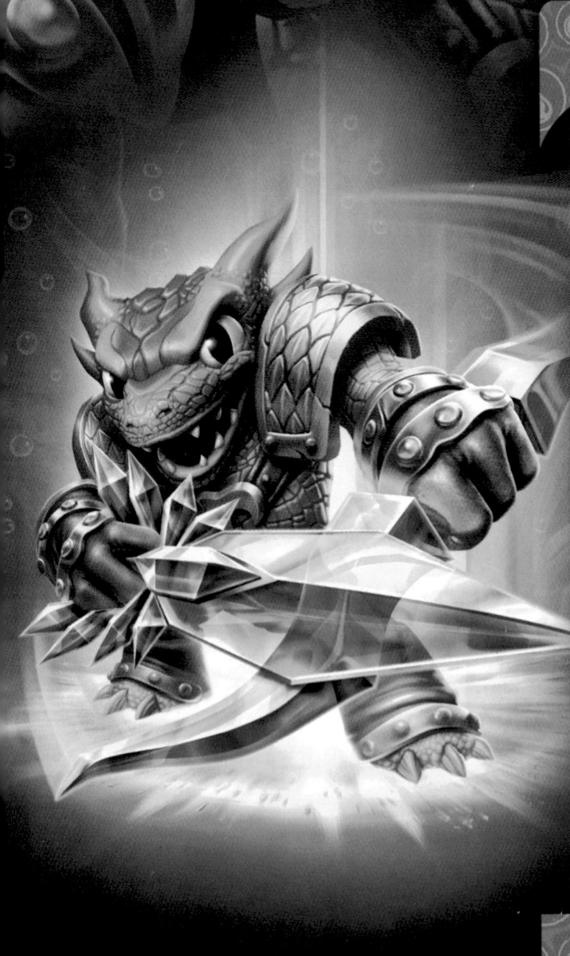

BIO

Snap Shot came from a long line of Crocagators that lived in the remote Swamplands, where he hunted chompies for sport. After rounding up every evil critter in his homeland, Snap Shot ventured out into the world to learn new techniques that he could use to track down more challenging monsters. He journeyed far and wide, perfecting his archery skills with the Elves and his hunting skills with the wolves. Soon he was the most revered monster hunter in Skylands—a reputation that caught the attention of Master Eon. It then wasn't long before Snap Shot became the leader of the Trap Masters, a fearless team of Skylanders that mastered legendary weapons made of pure Traptanium. It was this elite team that tracked down and captured the most notorious villains Skylands had ever known!

WALLOP

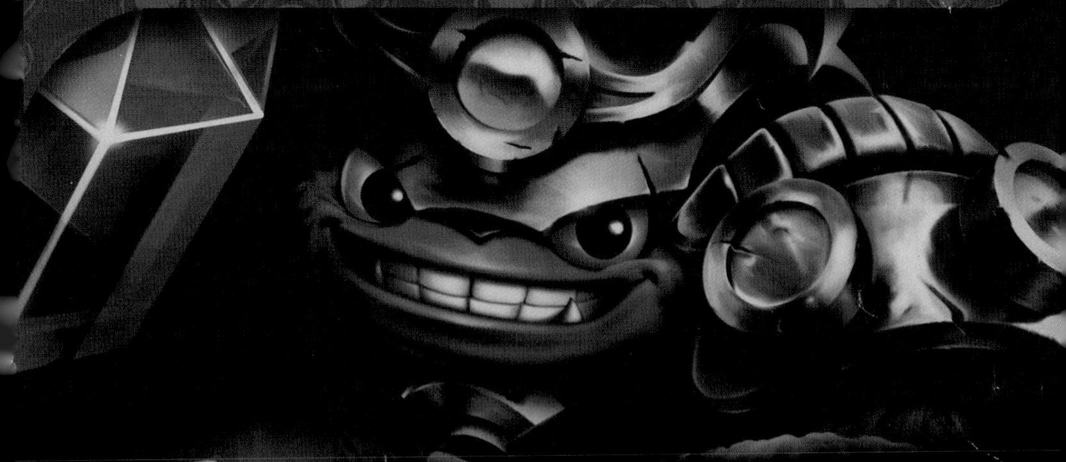

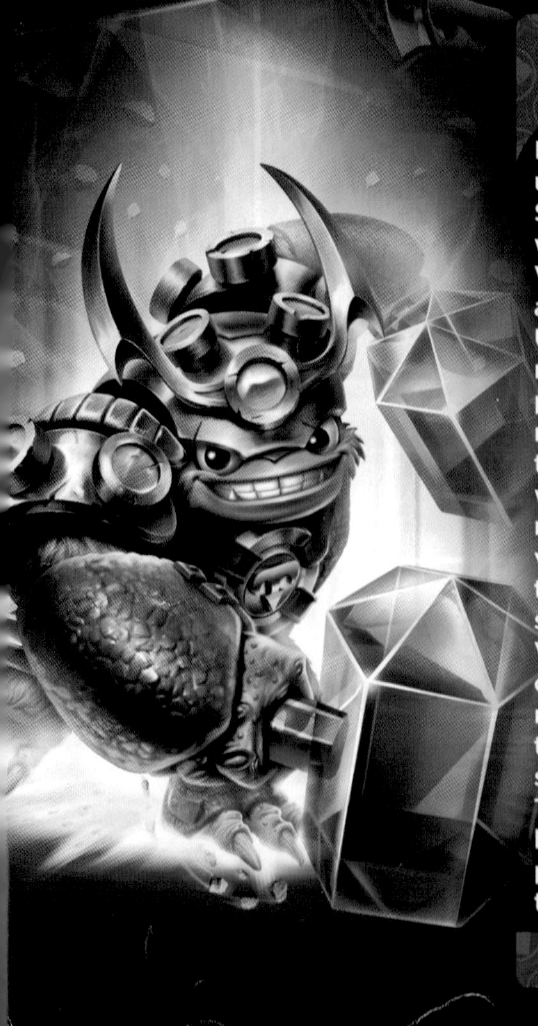

BIO

For generations, *Wallop's* people used the volcanic lava pits of Mount Scorch to forge the most awesome weapons in all of Skylands. And Wallop was the finest apprentice any of the masters had ever seen. Using hammers in both of his mighty hands, he could tirelessly pound and shape the incredibly hot metal into the sharpest swords or the hardest axes. But on the day he was to demonstrate his skills to the masters of his craft, a fierce fire viper awoke from his deep sleep in the belly of the volcano. The huge snake erupted forth, attacking Wallop's village. But by bravely charging the beast with his two massive hammers, Wallop was able to bring down the creature and save his village. Now with his Traptanium-infused hammers, he fights with the Skylanders to protect the lands from any evil that rises to attack!

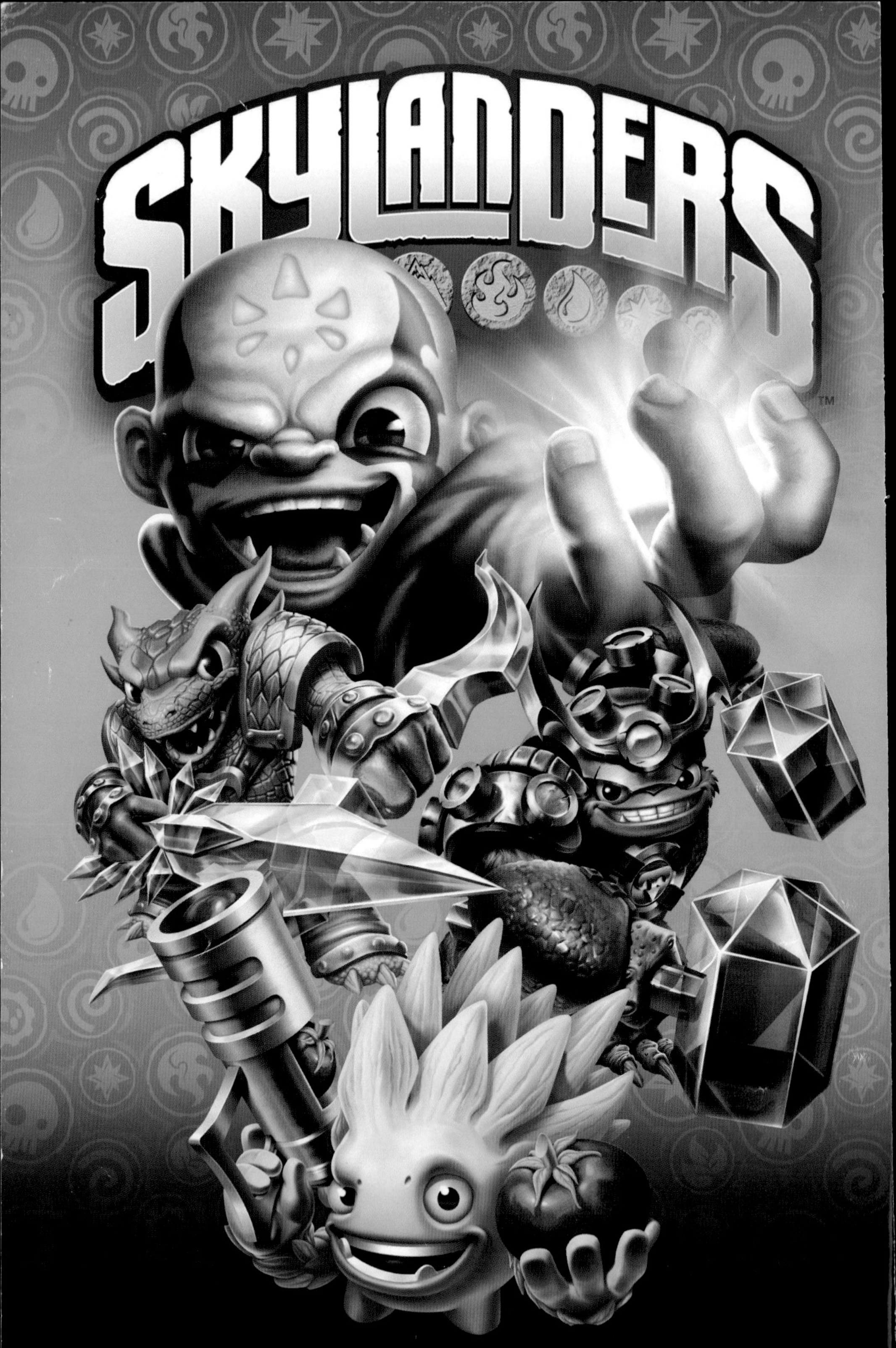
SKYLANDERS

THE KAOS TRAP